To my wife for ... ... support.

"The only absolute and best friend a man has, in this selfish world, the only one that will not betray or deny him, is his dog". It was first used by King Frederick II of Prussia before his death in 1786.

CONTENTS

The
Coronation Murders

Prologue

The date was Saturday, the 30th of May 1953, just three days before there was to be the coronation of the new monarch, Her Majesty Queen Elizabeth the Second, in Westminster Abbey.

The BBC's meteorologists had announced on the wireless this morning that the current inclement weather was due to an extensive low-pressure system being stuck over the British Isles and giving weather more akin to October than the end of May.

The leaded window panes of the ivy-clad Georgian Manor rattled as the unseasonal driving rain and wind lashed them. At the end of the timber-lined dining room in its iron grate, the log fire roared and hissed as the raindrops descended the ancient chimney, spitting black sooty spots upon the hearth.

From his position at the head of his highly polished oak dining table, the Brigadier looked around at the eight seated members of the society he had created, little knowing that before the end of the following month, two of the club would be dead and another injured.

The members were all residents of the Kent village of Lower Dipping, and though they came from varied walks of life, The one thing they all shared was their love of their dogs.

They had all met at one time or another whilst walking their pets. When the Brigadier came up with the idea of forming a club with his fellow dog lovers, they readily agreed.

But being the Brigadier, he thought that club was far too common a name for a gathering of such village worthies. He decided he would call them a society.

CHAPTER 1

The first meeting Of
The West Kent Dog Walkers Society

To the Brigadier's left, dressed in a checked Harris Tweed Jacket and skirt, sat the tall, fifty-something, grey-haired, no-nonsense headmistress of the local primary school, Miss Harlan. Being renowned for her austere manner and sharp tongue, it would have to be a fearless person who asked her what the something was.

To her left was seated Joe Ross, a thin, sharp-featured man in his mid-fifties with a pencil-line moustache dressed in a shiny pin-striped suit that had seen better days. Joe Ross, known as a spiv during the war, was now considered locally as a lovable rogue who classed himself as a general dealer.

Joe was not the sort of person that the Brigadier would generally have been seen dead with. Still, the Brigadier was wise enough to know that if there was ever something he wanted to do, Joe was the man to get it done, as he was known locally as the Mister Fix It.

Joe's house was an old, run-down, flint-faced cottage surrounded by equally run-down sheds on the outskirts of the village beside the stream which flooded his yard after every thunderstorm.

Next to Joe sat Bert Love, a broad-shouldered muscular ex-marine and landlord of the village's only watering hole, a public house named the Black Swan or, as the locals called it, the Mucky Duck, which he ran with the assistance of his formidable barmaid Elsie.

Seated opposite the Brigadier at the far end of the table sat Ophelia, his wife of the last forty years, who had followed and served alongside her husband throughout his army career in Africa and India.

She epitomised the very definition of the memsahib with her superior attitude to any that she considered not up to her social standing.

At her mistress's feet, sprawled on her pink velvet cushion beneath the table and giving the occasional snarl, lay Suki, Ophelia's bad-tempered Pomeranian.

Next to Ophelia sat the newly arrived vicar of Saint Mary's church, having only been in the village for three months along with his sister, Mary, who acted as his housekeeper and secretary.

The Reverend William Davis, or Bill Davis, as he was more commonly known in the village, was fair-haired and of slim build, which made him appear younger than his thirty-two years.

Mary, his younger sister, had her French mother's complexion and shoulder-length black hair that gave her a very Gallic appearance. And they lived in the old stone-built vicarage with its flint-covered walls and thatch roof.

Another pair of siblings took the last two seats: Doctor Anne Clements and her brother Ron, who were both single and lived at Lower Dipping House in the centre of the village.

Anne was an attractive, auburn-haired young woman in her late twenties and often seen driving around the parish in her black Hillman Minx, visiting her patients.

Her brother Ron was older by a couple of years and owned the local garage/smithy.

By any standards, he was a large man, even making Bert Love look puny by comparison.

Where Anne was slim and attractive, her brother stood well over six feet with broad shoulders and bulging biceps. He also had a scar running the length of his jaw and a patch covering the socket where his left eye had been.

Next to Ron, in what he saw as his rightful place at the head of the table, stood the Brigadier, framed by his two yellow labradors, Molly and Dolly. He looked dapper with his swept-back grey hair, dark blue blazer and snazzy silk cravat.

He finished his look at the members of the society rapped on the table for attention and said. "Welcome, ladies and gentlemen, on this foul afternoon to the first meeting of the West Kent

Dog Walkers Society."

Taking a deep breath, he continued. "I think the first order of business should be the coronation on Tuesday and what we can do to help prepare."

The vicar raised his hand and said. "I think, Brigadier, that the village coronation committee have got most of the arrangements in place. Joe has arranged a television for the village hall so anyone who wants to attend can watch the coronation."

Bert Love said with a smile. "Joe's been busy because he has also arranged another television for the pub."

Joe gave his shoulders a shrug and tapped the side of his bent nose with his finger.

"If this bad weather persists, the planned street party will have to be moved inside to the primary school hall and classrooms after the coronation." Said Miss Harlan.

"Ahem, maybe I can help you there. I know where to get a marquee if you think there isn't enough room in the school, Miss Harlan." Said Joe helpfully.

"Why thank you, Mr Ross, that is most kind of you, and I shall certainly mention it to the committee." Said Miss Harlan, giving an uncharacteristic smile.

The Brigadier got to his feet and, sounding slightly peeved at the stealing of his thunder, pointed to the rain rattling upon the windows, "Well, it appears the coronation committee seem to have it all in hand, and as there is nothing more to discuss. I suggest we fetch all the dogs for a walk around the grounds next week. But, neither the dogs nor any of us would appreciate it in this weather, so I will now call an end to today's meeting due to the weather and that we return here next Saturday when I hope the climate will be more temperate.

We can then discuss some activities we may take with the dogs to raise money for the community now if you all care to follow me to the library, where drinks await.

**

The visitors stood at the front door to the Manor, watching the rain bouncing off the driveway.

"Oh my, if I hadn't given Hopkins the day off, he could have taken you all home in my Rolls."

"I have my Hillman if you don't mind squeezing together?" Said Anne before dashing out into the rain without waiting for an answer to collect her car.

Bringing the car to a halt at the front door of the Manor, the wet doctor shouted, "Mary, you get in the back first, followed by Ron, Miss Harlan and then Bert. Vicar, you can sit beside me, followed by Joe."

Everyone piled into the car as instructed, and Miss Harlan, feeling squeezed between the two well-built men, said, "Ooh, I can't remember the last time I found myself pressed between two men."

Bert chuckled and said, "Miss Harlan, you must tell

us about your past some time."

Miss Harlan replied with a dirty chuckle, "Not on your Nelly Duff."

Anne turned to the vicar and said, "Good job, this car has a column gear stick, or I might grab your knee by accident." The rest of the passengers laughed at Bill's scarlet face as the car pulled away from the Manor.

***

The first passenger Anne dropped off was Joe Ross. Joe's house was an old, run-down, flint-faced cottage surrounded by equally run-down sheds on the outskirts of the village beside the stream which flooded his yard after every thunderstorm.

At the window stood Rex awaiting his master; Rex was an elderly King Charles spaniel with a bad habit of quietly breaking wind caused by eating any garbage he could find lying around Joe's cottage yard. The smell didn't affect Joe in the least because of the broken nose he had acquired in his youth, which had caused him to lose his sense of smell, but not so any other unfortunate person in the room. With agility belying his age, Joe leapt from the car. And, with a backwards wave splashed through the puddles and into his house.

***

Miss Harlan was next to be dropped off; who complained that she was pretty comfortable where she was and wouldn't mind being last.

Unfortunately for her, her cottage was next in line, and Bert gallantly got out to escort her to her door, where Albie, her Harlequin great-dane, greeted her with a flurry of slobbering licks as if he hadn't seen her for three days instead of three hours.

***

Bert returned to the car and said that due to his gallantry, he was soaking wet and would walk the two hundred yards to his pub and take Jake, his Irish wolfhound, for a walk.

When anyone first met Jake, his appearance gave the impression that he wanted to rip out the nearest person's throat, which was a good deterrent against any would-be troublemakers in the pub.

In reality, anyone who knew him would be aware that he was the most good-natured dog in the room and also, on the quiet, a bit of a coward.

***

Anne's final drop off before heading home was Bill and Mary Davis at the vicarage.

During the war and before joining the clergy, Bill had, at only twenty-four years of age, been one of the ten thousand paratroopers dropped into Arnhem in the ill-fated attempt to capture and hold the bridge until reinforcements arrived. After nine days of fierce fighting, he had been one of the lucky two thousand nine hundred men who had managed to escape after the battle by crossing the river back to the Allied lines.

Bill was not the only one in the family fighting the Germans. During the war, Mary, due to her Gallic appearance and her ability to speak fluent French, had served in the SOE and had been one of the forty-one female agents in the famous F section.

She had been parachuted into France and had worked and fought alongside the French Maquis against the Germans for a year and a half up until the end of the war.

She had considered herself fortunate to have survived her missions into occupied France, unlike sixteen of her fellow female agents who had perished, some enduring excruciating torture at the hands of the Gestapo before being executed.

As Bill and Mary opened the door to the vicarage, their two dogs, Duchess and Tilly, nearly bowled them over. Duchess, a golden retriever, normally behaved with a calm demeanour, while Tilly, being a springer spaniel, was manic at all times.

***

Anne and Ron arrived at Lower Dipping House, laughing at Miss Harlan's behaviour in the car.

"I think she had one sherry too many at the Brigadiers." Said Ron, opening the front door to be met by the rush of their two dogs.

After the war, whilst in London to see his surgeon in connection with the injuries he had received on Sword Beach during the D-Day invasion, he had discovered a half-starved one-eared puppy with a black patch over her left eye scavenging for food amongst the rubble of a bomb site.

When she approached to lick his hand, he felt an immediate affinity with this scarred and starving dog and decided that there was nothing he could do but name her Bonny and take her back home with him to Lower Dipping.

Ron had received his injuries in a grenade blast whilst attacking an enemy pillbox and, despite his injuries, continued with his attack, destroying the pillbox before becoming overcome by his wounds.

He had been mentioned in dispatches for this action and later awarded the Military Medal for bravery.

Anne's dog, Archie, was a blue roan cocker spaniel. And though Archie had the gentlest of dispositions and loved being fussed, he had one problem: his breath. It was so bad some people unkindly said it could strip paint.

Amos Tennent, the Brigadier's gamekeeper, had suggested diluting some apple cider vinegar in Archie's water bowl. This remedy, however, had only helped a little, so she now had resorted to cleaning Archie's teeth with a toothbrush once a week.

During the war, Anne had been undergoing her training as a doctor in London where, though not yet qualified, she and her other trainees were often called upon by senior doctors to help with the civilians injured in the nighttime bombings.

CHAPTER 2

Coronation Day
Tuesday Morning

The big day arrived, and the village of Lower Dipping was a hive of activity from nine in the morning with women carrying trays of spam and fish paste sandwiches, cakes and bowls of jelly into the school hall, where they were laid out neatly on the trestle tables alongside the paper hats and bottles of fizzy drinks ready for the children after the coronation.

The weather wasn't as bad as Saturday, but June was still very cool and damp. It was a good job Joe had delivered on his promise of a marquee erected the previous day by a gang of unknown men covering the school playground so that the swings and the slide would be kept dry in the event of rain, thus keeping the children amused.

In the public bar of the Black Swan, watched by his bemused dog Jake, Bert Love was cursing as he tried to get a watchable picture on his hired television.

"Lift it higher." Snapped Bert to his barmaid holding the aerial.

"You want this aerial any bleeding higher; you better find a taller barmaid." Elsie retorted.

"Don't tempt me," Muttered Bert under his breath.

"If we moved the set closer to the window, we might get a better picture?" Suggested Bert.

"You can bloody move it then." Answered an irritated Elsie as she tossed the aerial into the corner.

"That's it; you've done it, you clever girl. A perfect picture". An excited Bert said, hugging Elsie as she came across to see the screen.

"Is that all it does?" Asked Elsie.

"No, according to Joe, that is what they call a test card to ensure you get a good picture." Said Bert. "Now, let's leave it alone and go and have a drink."

Along the street from Mucky Duck in the village hall, Mary and the vicar had finished setting up their television when the door crashed open, and a greasy, long-haired young man in his early twenties with a camera slung around his neck entered.

"Wotcha, vicar," He said, lifting his camera. "Take your picture, Mary?"

"No, you will not, Micky," said Bill, stepping before his sister, whom he had seen clenching her fist, ready to strike if the young man had come any closer. "Now, what do you want?"

"I've come to watch the coronation and take a few photos. I wanted to sit near the front, so I decided to arrive early.

"Micky, you're wrong on both counts. One, the

seats at the front are for the old folk of the village to get a better view of the proceedings and two, you will only be taking photos with people's permission. Is that understood?"

Micky approached the vicar with a swagger and stood with his face two inches from the vicar. "And who is going to stop me? You."

"Micky, just because I'm wearing a dog collar, do not think I'm going to be intimidated by a useless pile of shit like you," Bill whispered in Micky's ear whilst placing his hand on the younger man's shoulder before grabbing a handful of greasy locks and twisting.

Micky let out a yell of pain and started to buckle at the knees as Bill steered him forcefully towards the door past the smiling Mary.

"Now out you go, Micky and don't come back until you know how to behave," He said, giving Micky a shove that sent the long-haired lout sprawling into the street.

"Everything all right, Bill?" Asked Ron Clements as the flying Micky landed at the feet of him and his sister as they were making their way past the hall on their way to the school.

The smiling Bill chuckled and said. "Just clearing some rubbish out of the hall."

"I'll get the police on you for assault." Spluttered Micky from his position in the gutter. "And you better not have damaged my camera."

"Micky, it must be your lucky day, for here comes our new village, Bobby," said a smiling Ron.

PC Dave Gregory was a tall, slim officer in his early twenties who had joined the Kent Constabulary upon completing his national service. Lower Dipping was his first posting, where he was one of the two constables, the other being Jack Day, a lugubrious man in his mid-forties who did as little work as possible and was killing time until retirement. They were both supervised by the overweight Sergeant Wilson, who, similar to Jack Day, was doing as little as possible whilst awaiting his retirement.

Looking down at Micky with dislike showing upon his face, he said. "Why are you lying there, Micky?"

"He threw me out of the hall and into the gutter." Said Micky, pointing at Bill.

"Is that true, vicar?" Asked the policeman.

"Yes," He replied.

"Did he cause a disturbance in the hall?"

"He was very argumentative, so I showed him to the door when he tripped upon leaving," Bill said, keeping a straight face.

"That's true, officer. My sister and I saw it all as we were passing." Said Ron, indicating the doctor.

"They're all lying," Micky said in a shrill voice of desperation. "He threw me into the gutter."

"Are you telling me that a vicar, a doctor and a respected businessman are all lying and that I should believe you? Get to your feet, Micky and go home before I arrest you for behaviour likely to cause a breach of the peace." With that, he leaned over the recumbent Micky and, grabbing him by the greasy collar of his jacket, dragged him to his feet and propelled him toward the pre-fabs on the outskirts of the village where he lived with his blowsy mother.

"Thank you for your assistance, constable, and hope we will see you later at the party at the school," Ron said.

"I'm on duty, but I'm certain to be on patrol near the tea party." He smiled as he gave a touch to the rim of his helmet in a one-fingered salute before he continued on his beat.

Come eleven o'clock, Lower Dipping appeared to be a ghost town with all its deserted streets.

The villagers were all either in their homes listening to the coronation on their wirelesses or watching televisions, specially hired for the occasion.

In the village hall, the seats were all filled with the older parishioners in the front row staring at the black-and-white picture on the screen.

The children's mothers had all instructed their children sitting on the floor at the front to behave, or there would be no party.

The Black Swan public bar was similarly packed, with men seated at the bar and tables watching the grainy picture on the television.

"Oh, she looks so young." Exclaimed Elsie to her husband George as she pulled him a pint of best bitter whilst giving a glance towards the television.

Taking a sip of his pint, George said. "Yep, you

know she's only twenty-seven and had Elsie read in today's Express that New Zealand mountaineer Edmund Hilary and Sherpa Tenzing had conquered Everest for the first time in history."

"Well, you are a mine of information today, aren't you," replied his wife.

"That's what comes of reading an intellectual paper like the Daily Express."

Laughing, Elsie said. "Come off it, George. I know you only buy it to follow the adventures of Rupert, the bear."

CHAPTER 3

Coronation Day
Tuesday Afternoon

At the end of three hours, the coronation had come to its end, and all the children who had sat patiently throughout the ceremony stampeded from their houses and the village hall towards the school, where the villagers had laid out the food and drink on the trestle tables under the supervision of Miss Harlan.

The noise in the school was deafening, with excited children fighting for seats at the tables and the adults discussing the coronation when there was a sudden clanging of the school bell, which brought the hall to a startled silence.

Embarrassed, Mary lowered the bell and said. "I always wanted to do that, but my brother would like to say a short prayer of thanks."

After the short prayer, the party began. The children tucked into the food with gusto, and the village ladies discussed the coronation. And how beautiful the young queen had looked in her elaborate robes.

Bill and Ron leaned on the makeshift bar, holding

their beer bottles and looking around the room at the celebrating villagers.

Bill said, "That pile of food soon disappeared; nothing remains except that plate of rock cakes, which nobody wants to eat."

Ron laughed and said, "Do you want to know why?" Bill gave a nod of his head. "All the locals know that Anne baked them; she has many skills, but cooking is not one of them. Last year, the Women's Institute had a baking competition to raise money, and poor Mrs Osbourne, your predecessor's housekeeper acting as judge, broke a tooth on one of Anne's rock cakes."

The Brigadier and Ophelia wandered around the hall like minor royalty, shaking hands with some of their estate workers and handing the children paper bags of homemade sweets. Ophelia would not have lowered herself to make sweets; that would have been down to their cook, Mrs Moore, up at the Manor.

Kathy Jordan, Micky's mother, turned on the wireless and shouted over the noise. "Let's get this party started."

People were soon dancing to the big band music in the classrooms and outside in the marquee.

The adults and some children danced in the school hall while Mr Lee and his sons supervised other children taking pony rides around the village green.

Mr Lee and his family were Romanys and, annually, camped in the field owned by Joe Ross alongside the stream at the edge of the woods whilst working on the local farms and carrying out odd jobs around the village. They had been coming to Lower Dipping for so many years that they were almost considered locals, with their children attending the local school.

After the first hour of the party, Mary gathered the empty cups and plates and told Miss Harlan. "I'll just take these back to the Vicarage and get them washed."

"Don't be too long, dear. The party's just getting warmed up." Said the grey-haired headmistress, giving a hiccup. "I think I had better ease up on the sherry."

Threading her way carefully between the puddles, thankful that the rain was staying away, Mary arrived at the vicarage's back door to discover the door standing ajar and the glass in the window broken.

Quietly placing the cups and plates on the lawn so as not to disturb the intruder who may still be inside, she ran back to the school to find her brother, little realising that she was being watched from the shelter of the marquee by a smiling cold-eyed killer.

Seeing his sister's face as she rushed into the school, Bill crossed the room to discover what was wrong.

When told about the broken window, he joined Ron and Bert, who were chatting at the makeshift bar and told them of Mary's discovery.

Before setting off to investigate, Bill said to his sister, "Go to the police house and see if you can find PC Gregory and tell him what you found; in the meantime, we will see if anyone is still at the vicarage."

Arriving at the vicarage, Bill said. "If you two enter through the front, I will come in from the back, and hopefully, we will catch any intruder between us and by all means, feel free to bash anyone that looks like a burglar."

"Will he be wearing a mask with a striped jumper and carrying a bag marked swag?" Smiled Bert.

After giving the other two a few minutes head start, he stepped carefully around the tray of crockery on the lawn. Gently pushing open the door to the kitchen, trying not to step on the broken glass, he made his way through the house to the hallway.

Light shone into the dark hallway as Ron and Bert opened the front door to reveal a dark shape at the foot of the stairs.

"It appears your young friend Micky Jordan decided to look around while you were out?" Said Bert, indicating the still form on the floor.

Kneeling beside the body, Bill pressed his fingers to the side of Micky's neck in search of a pulse.

Getting back to his feet, he said to Ron. "I can't find any pulse. Could you bring your sister over to confirm that Micky is dead?"

On his way out, Ron passed PC Gregory in the doorway, "Well, vicar, it looks as if Micky thought he would pay you a visit whilst you were busy at the party."

"That is the consensus we have come to; where is my sister?"

"I told her to wait outside until I was certain it was safe for her

to come in."

The vicar smiled and didn't say that Mary could defend herself if the need should arise but appreciated the policeman's gallantry.

PC Gregory looked at the body and how it was lying before saying. "It looks like he tripped at the top of the stairs and fell."

Turning to two men, he said. "I think this is just an unfortunate accident and that he died from a broken neck whilst trying to rob your house."

"And when did you get your medical degree, constable?" Said a female voice from the open door.

Turning to see who had spoken, PC Gregory saw Anne Clements standing with her brother and holding her medical bag.

Red-faced, the policeman said, "I'm sorry, doctor. I should have said that he appears to be dead from a possible broken neck."

Anne smiled, saying nothing more crossed to the body, and began her examination.

After ten minutes, she stood up and smiled at the policeman. "You were correct in your diagnosis in so far as that he is dead, but I don't think he died of a broken neck, but a blow to his throat judging by bruising."

"Maybe he hit his throat on the edge of the step as he fell from the landing." Said Gregory in an attempt to save face.

"I don't think he was up the stairs at any time," the vicar remarked.

"What makes you think that?" Snapped the young policeman, who was beginning to get rattled that these people were dismissing all his ideas.

Bill answered in a conciliatory tone. "We agree that he came in through the kitchen door?" To which Gregory nodded. "Coming in from the garden, Micky left a muddy trail through the kitchen and into the hallway. Looking at the soles of his shoes, they still have a covering of mud, but there is no mud on the stairs."

PC Gregory looked up at the clean stairs, nodded, and said.

"That being the case, it appears that he was killed in the hallway, which would indicate there was someone else here, thus making it a possible murder scene. So I must ask you to leave the premises while I report back to Sergeant Wilson, who will have to contact his superiors in Maidstone."

"I'm glad the dogs were with us," Bill said, patting his retriever's head. "Goodness knows what Micky might have done to them if he had found them in the house."

After PC Gregory had left to report to Sergeant Wilson, Anne placed an arm around Mary's shoulders and said. "There is plenty of room at our place; you and Bill must stay with us for as long as the vicarage is closed off by the police."

Before the police returned to usher them from their house, they rushed around, filling a bag with a few personal items along with the dogs' dishes. They went to Ron and Anne's home, Lower Dipping House, where they left Duchess and Tilly with Bonny and Archie in the walled garden before returning to the school.

As they entered, Miss Harlan and Joe came across to enquire what was happening, as PC Day had come in and, under the curious stares of the partygoers, escorted Mrs Jordan from the room.

Ron informed them of their discovery at the vicarage, causing Miss Harlan to sit at a table while Bert went to the bar for more drinks.

CHAPTER 4

Coronation Day
Tuesday Evening

Later, at the Black Swan, they found the public bar packed with villagers still celebrating by dancing the conga around the tables.

Over the heads of her customers, Elsie waved her hand, indicating that they made their way into the saloon bar where the rest of the West Kent Dog Walkers Society were seated around a cluster of copper-topped tables.

"Come and take a seat," said the Brigadier. "I'll get you some drinks. Brandies all around, I think."

"What mischief do you think that young bounder was up to at your home?" The Brigadier asked the vicar, who had gone from brandy to a pint of Courages best bitter.

"Whatever it was, Brigadier, you can be certain that he was up to no good, and there is something I want you all to see," he said, taking the letter from his pocket and spreading it on the table.

"It's from my predecessor, the Reverend Peters, and it arrived soon after my arrival in the village to warn me about Micky Jordan."

Dear Reverend Davis,

I am sending this letter to warn you about a member of your new parish.
Shortly before my retirement, a family friend who resided in the village told me he had been approached by Micky Jordan, demanding fifty pounds in return for photos he had taken of their teenage daughter in various stages of undress.
It appears he had convinced the girl, who was young for her age, that he loved her and if she loved him in return, she should allow him to take her photographs. If they failed to comply with his demands or told the police, he would post pictures of their daughter around the village and ruin the girl's reputation.
The girl's father had paid the money to Micky in return for the negatives before removing his family from the village to another county to avoid any possible scandal.
The one thing the girl's father did before leaving was to tell me what Micky had done so that I could keep an eye on Micky to stop it from happening again to another unfortunate girl.
I am telling you this so that you may also keep an eye on this despicable young man and prevent him from doing further harm.

Yours faithfully,

David Peters

"I always thought he was a nasty little bugger." Ron said, "But he was even nastier than I thought. Are you going to show this letter to the police?"

"I suppose I'll have to," Bill said. "But what if the girl's father killed him?"

"That's not for you to decide, old boy. It's a job for a judge and jury." Stated the Brigadier.

"I suppose, being a man of God vicar, you would have turned the other cheek and forgiven him if you had discovered him in your house?" Asked Ophelia in her drawling tones.

"I'm uncertain as to how I would have reacted had I met him in my house, but I shall still pray for his eternal soul, and now, if you will all excuse me, I must go and offer my condolences to Micky's poor mother." And picking up the letter from the table, headed for the door.

***

As the early evening sun attempted to break through the dark rain clouds, the vicar approached the front door to Kathy Jordan's prefab, his mind racing as he thought about what he would say to the poor woman.

As he raised his fist to rap on the front door with its green flaking paint, it suddenly opened and startled PC Gregory.

"Good grief, vicar, what a fright you gave me. I

thought you would punch me in the nose for one minute." Said the smiling young policeman.

"Oh, I'm so sorry, Constable," said the vicar, lowering his hand. "Is it okay for me to go in and speak with Mrs Jordan?"

"Be my guest vicar, but she's in a pretty bad way. She has been on the gin since she heard of Micky's death.

You will also be pleased to hear that the CID has arrived from Maidstone, and when they have finished, you can move back into your home."

"Thank you, constable, but I don't think we will move back in today, as my sister will want to give the place a thorough scrub even though there was no blood."

"As you wish, reverend. I just thought you may like to know, and the detectives will be along to see you later for a statement." Said Gregory, leaving the vicar alone on the doorstep.

Entering the dark hallway, he felt the soles of his shoes sticking to the dirty linoleum floor as he made his way to what he assumed was the sitting room.

How do people live like this, he said to himself. Giving a call of "Hello Mrs Jordan, it's me, Reverend Davis," he opened the sitting-room door to discover Kathy Jordan slumped unconscious in an armchair with an empty gin bottle tucked at her side next to the arm of the chair, whilst on the floor where It had landed, lay her glass.

Bill's eyes settled on a stack of photographic

magazines he assumed belonged to Micky, piled neatly beside the threadbare sofa.

The fire grate was empty except for the charred remains of what had once been some black and white photographs.

Kneeling beside the fire, he gently raked through the still-warm ash and found the bottom of the one photo that remained; it showed what looked like two pairs of men's feet among some trees.

He decided that while he was in the house, it wouldn't hurt to look around and see what Micky had been up to with the camera he always carried.

Leaving the sitting room and entering the hall, the first door he opened appeared to be Kathy's bedroom, with her clothes strewn about the room. Closing the door behind him, he opened the next door, which was the bathroom and toilet. He smiled to himself as the bath was half full of coal, and it reminded him of his grandad who, after moving into a new house with indoor plumbing, had used the tub to store coal and bathed in a tin bath in front of the coal fire. When asked why he didn't use the new indoor facilities, he said the bathroom was too cold. That would not be a problem in this bathroom, though, as a paraffin heater stood in the corner.

Fortunately, the toilet was just a toilet, though it would have benefited from a bottle of bleach poured around the bowl.

The third door he opened must have been Micky's room, which was surprisingly tidy for such a slob.

Micky had made his bed and stacked his books on photography on a corner shelf before leaving that morning, little knowing that he would not be returning.

The pictures on his wall were ones that Micky had taken around the village of the cottages and the old woodland beside the stream with its ancient oak trees. He admired one, in particular; it was of an old gnarled oak standing proudly in a clearing with the sun shining through its twisted branches. Looking over the photographs, he thought Micky had a good eye for detail and was naturally talented.

It was such a pity he had wasted his natural-born ability on blackmail.

Looking around the room, he assumed Micky must have a darkroom in the house to develop his film as he was unlikely to send his film containing images of half-naked young ladies to the chemist shop in Swanley to get his photographs printed.

Putting his head through the final doorway, all there was to see was the kitchen with its dirty pans and plates stacked in the sink.

After glancing into the sitting room to check that Kathy Jordan hadn't choked on her vomit, he exited the house and turned toward the pub, closing the front door behind him.

He had only taken a half dozen strides when he suddenly thought if the coal was in the bath, what was in the coal shed at the back of the prefab.

With a quick about-turn, he went to the rear of the

house to find the door to the coal shed sporting a large padlock.

"Bugger!" He exclaimed and gave the door a hefty kick in frustration.

To his surprise, the padlock sprung open and fell to the ground.

Giving a glance skywards, he gave a whisper of. "Thank you, Lord."

Entering the room was an anti-climax. On the workbench was an expensive-looking enlarger for shining the images onto the photographic paper, a tank for developing film sitting beside two trays for developing and fixing the photographs.

Disgusted that he couldn't find any incriminating photographs hanging to dry, he left the darkroom, padlocking the door behind me, and returned to the party in the Mucky Duck.

"Just in time to buy a round," was his greeting upon arrival at the saloon bar.

While he had been away, the West Kent Dog Walkers Society had been drinking steadily to Her Majesty's good health and long reign.

Putting his hand around the vicar's shoulders, Ron said. "Don't let Micky Jordan ruin a good party. He wasn't worth it; now come and sit next to Anne while I get you a drink."

CHAPTER 5

Coronation Night
Tuesday/Wednesday

It was three AM when the four dogs shattered the quiet of Lower Dipping House, as the fire engine's bell set them to barking on its race through the centre of the village towards the burning building. Ron raced from his room in time to meet Anne and Mary coming from Anne's room.

Bill had been sleeping on the sofa down the stairs in the lounge and was shouting at all the dogs to be quiet as he untangled himself from his blankets.

The others arrived downstairs, and he was preparing to run out of the front door when Mary, Anne and Ron let out a chorus of "Stop."

"Why?" Bill answered sharply.

Ron grinned and said. "You're not wearing your dog collar."

"What are you on about?" He asked, turning to face the others.

"Ron is trying to tell you that you're not wearing trousers discreetly." Giggled Anne and Mary.

"Just imagine what the local gossip would say if the vicar left the lady doctor's house in the middle of the night minus his trousers.

That could be the headline story in next Sunday's News of the World." Ron Laughed.

Looking down at his bare legs, he felt his face redden and was glad of the semi-darkness before dashing back to reclaim his trousers from the back of the sofa.

Once they were all suitably attired and the girls had finally stopped giggling, they made their way through the village with several other villagers, heading towards the plume of smoke rising into the night sky.

Upon their arrival at the burning house, Mary said. "Oh, dear God, whose house is that?"

"It's Kathy Jordan's house where I was earlier," Bill said as two firemen played their hoses onto the smouldering flat roof of the prefab.

Suddenly, two more firemen appeared through the smoke, carrying the limp form of Kathy Jordan between them before laying her on the pavement.

Anne ran forward with her medical bag, announcing to the firefighters that she was a doctor and began to search for any signs of life.

After a few minutes, Anne stood up, closed her bag, and told the fireman. "I'm sorry to say I can do nothing more as she is dead. Do you have anything with which I may cover the body?"

The fireman went to the engine to get a tarp, and Mary said. "How can she be dead if she has no burns?"

"It would have been the smoke that killed her," Bill

answered.

"But, it wasn't." Anne interrupted. "I cannot be certain how she died, but I'm pretty certain I could feel her crushed skull caused by a severe blow to the back of her head through her hair."

As the crowd gathered, all three village policemen arrived.

Dave Gregory was the first to arrive and was, as always, smartly turned out even though it was the middle of the night.

The second to arrive on the scene, the opposite of Dave Gregory, wearing his rumpled uniform and scuffed shoes, was PC Jack Day.

The overweight Sergeant Humphrey Wilson was the last to arrive, puffing from the exertion of his fast waddle from the police house.

"Gregory, Day, get these people back from the fire engine," ordered the panting sergeant.

Turning to one of the firemen, he said," I suppose the body under the tarp died from smoke inhalation?"

The fireman turned to the pompous sergeant with a smile and said, "Not according to the doctor; she said the woman died from a blow to the back of her head."

"Bugger." the sergeant muttered under his breath, turned to Anne in the small crowd, and said. "Doctor, thank you for your assistance, but how certain are you about the cause of death?"

"Pretty confident, sergeant, as it appears she has a crushed skull, though the pathologist will determine the cause of death at the post-mortem. To me, it looks as though you have another murder to deal with. Now, sergeant, if there is nothing else I can help you with, I think I shall go home and back to my bed." Anne said, turning away.

The sergeant huffed and puffed but managed to say. "Thank you," to the doctor's retreating figure.

CHAPTER 6

Coronation Day Plus 1
Wednesday

The quiet of the early morning at Lower Dipping House was again broken by the dogs barking, but this time, the cause was a hammering on the front door.

Picking his way through the pack of clamouring dogs, Ron opened the door to find two men in dark blue suits and trilby hats on the doorstep, accompanied by PC Gregory.

"Good morning, Mr Clements; this is Inspector Doyle and Sergeant Cornwell from the police headquarters in Maidstone, and they would like to ask you and your sister about the deaths of Kathy Jordan and her son Michael." Said a nervous PC, Gregory.

"Thank you, Constable; that will be all for now. If you could go back to the station and finish your report on the two deaths, it would be a great help." The Inspector kindly said to the anxious PC.

Ron showed the detectives to the lounge, where Mary, Anne and Bill sat on the sofa.

"Ahh, that's handy you all being here; maybe you

can apprise me of the events leading up to and including the deaths of Mrs Kathy Jordan and her son Michael. Starting with you, Miss Davis, as you discovered the body of Michael Jordan." The Inspector said before sitting in an armchair facing Mary while the sergeant stood behind him taking notes.

"To be precise, inspector, I discovered the broken window, and it was my brother, along with Mr Clements and Mr Love, who discovered the body."

After they had all gone through the happenings of the previous day and night, the sergeant had pocketed his notebook.

"There is just one more thing, inspector." Said the vicar and, removing his predecessor's letter from his pocket, handed it to the Inspector.

After reading the letter, the Inspector tucked it into his inside jacket pocket, got to his feet, looked sternly at the group sitting on the sofa, and said.

"That will be all for now, and if I have any further questions, I shall be in touch. First, though, I will have to speak with this Reverend David Peters and get the name of this girl's family and where I can find them."

After Ron had shown the Inspector and his sergeant to the door, they all let out a collective whoosh of breath.

"He seemed very friendly initially, and I thought he was charming." Said Mary. "But after you gave him the letter, his attitude changed."

"I'm glad I didn't show him the piece of the burnt

photograph I had found in the grate of Kathy Jordan's house as I think he might have dragged me off to the station as a suspect," said Bill.

"What picture is that?" Asked Ron.

Bill reached into his trouser pocket and held the charred photograph to show the others.

Ron said," Can't tell much from that.

"I don't know." Said Anne. "Wait a minute," and she disappeared into her study to return with a large pearl-handled magnifying glass.

"Aha!" Exclaimed Ron. "It's my sister Sherlock Anne, and now the game's afoot or should I say four feet."

Anne gave her brother a withering look as she held the magnifying glass over the remains of the picture.

Ron said, "As I said, not a lot to see."

"Well, we can see two pairs of feet facing each other, standing almost toe to toe," Bill observed.

"Those look to be men's shoes." Stated Mary.

"When people are talking to each other, they would never stand that close." Said Anne.

"So why are they standing that close?" Asked Mary.

"They would only stand that close if they were embracing or kissing," Bill said.

"But it looks to be two men judging by the style of their shoes." Said Mary innocently.

With raised eyebrows, Ron said. "That would be just the sort of picture Micky would take if he found these two in the woods, and it gave him a chance of the blackmail."

"Oh," said Mary as the penny dropped. "I wonder who they are?"

"I don't know," Bill said. "But I bet they will be glad that Micky is dead."

"Maybe it was one of them who killed him." Remarked Ron

Anne asked Bill, "Where do you think that is from?" He gave the photograph a closer look through the magnifying glass. "At a guess, I would say it's in the old oak wood down by the stream because if you look closely, you can just make out the willow trees that grow over the water, and when I was looking around Micky's house there were several pictures he had taken of the woods so it proves it was an area he frequented."

Stepping away from the photograph, Bill said. "If there are any clues as to who is in the picture, they will be in those woods, so that's where we have to look if we want to find the killer."

"Err, when did you discover you were the Anglican version of Father Brown?" Asked Ron.

"When they left a body at the bottom of the stairs in my home."

"Yes, I can understand how that would be rather irksome." Ron Smiled. "But now I have a business to run, so I'm off to work."

"I'm off to the surgery, but if you want to stay, make yourselves at home," Anne said before grabbing her medical bag and following her brother.

"Well," said Bill to his sister. "Are you coming back

to the vicarage with me?"

"I suppose I'll have to as I've nowhere else to live, but I'll tell you one thing. The first thing I will do is give that hall floor a good wash."

CHAPTER 7

Fisticuffs
Friday

Ron Clements was standing in the doorway of the Smithy, lost in thought and watching the world go by. Bill Davis was delivering the weekly parish newsletters to the village shop for Dave Edmands to put out for delivery with the paperboy in the morning, and Bert Love was outside his pub cleaning the windows.

As the roaring of six motorcycles broke Ron's trance, he let out a "bugger," They circled the war memorial in the square three times before coming to a halt outside the Mucky Duck.

Ron looked across the square towards Bert, who gave a nod, turned and entered the pub while Ron entered the Smithy.

***

Friday was Bill's day for delivering the parish newsletters, and while he and the owner of the village shop Dave Edmands, were having a chin wag over the counter, there was a roaring of motorcycle engines from the street.

"Uh oh," said Dave, looking through his shop window, "this could be trouble."

"What do you mean?"

"It was last year before you arrived, a gang of half a dozen motorcyclists ran riot in the village, causing no end of damage, and this looks like the same crowd.

"Did nobody try and stop them?"

"Ron Clements and Bert Love did try and got badly beaten for their trouble."

"Didn't the police do anything?"

"That tub of lard, they call a sergeant, and the gutless misery PC Day locked themselves in the police house until the bikers had left."

Looking through the shop window, Bill saw PC Gregory approaching the bikers with a determined set to his jaw.

"Uh oh, I think they have eventually got a policeman with balls; if you excuse my language, I will have to go out there."

Looking around the shop, he spied a bundle of broom handles in a tub in the corner.

"Dave, I almost forgot, I need a new broom handle for the vicarage. Can you please put this one on my account?"

Picking the sturdiest broom handle from the bundle, the vicar said farewell and headed toward the approaching Constable.

"Good afternoon, constable," He said steadily, "do you mind if I walk with you?"

The policeman broke stride and stopped, facing

the vicar. "That may not be a good idea at the moment, vicar, as I am just about to go and have a word with those leather-clad gentlemen standing over there."

"That is the very reason I wish to walk with you, as the sight of my dog collar may lighten the proceedings."

Gregory smiled and said, "It's your choice, vicar, but if things turn nasty, I hope you know how to look after yourself."

"Don't you worry about me and call me Bill as most of the village do, and by the way, I was informed a few minutes ago that this gang were here last year when they beat up Bert Love from the pub and my friend Ron Clements."

"That's interesting to know, as the sergeant forgot to mention that when he sent me up here to check their driving licences, my name is Dave in case you should need me in a hurry as it's shorter and quicker to say than Constable Gregory."

They approached the bikers, who spread out with the policeman and vicar in the centre, looking threatening.

"Good afternoon, constable, vicar; how can we help you?" Said the tall ginger-haired individual whom the PC and Bill assumed to be the gang's leader.

Bill gave Dave Gregory his due, as he gave no sign of being unsettled by the six leather-clad bikers, and approached the leader.

"As you have drawn such attention to yourselves

with your noisy arrival in the village, I would like you all to show me your driving licences, and while you are fetching them from your pockets, I will just take note of the registration numbers of your bikes." He then took his notebook from his breast pocket, licked the end of his pencil and began writing.

"And what will you do if we don't want to show you our licences?" Said Ginger, puffing out his chest and taking a step forward.

Pausing in his writing, PC Gregory looked him in the eye and calmly said. "I will just have to take you to the police house, where you will have to stay until we have checked your bike registrations and discovered your names."

"Ginger, let's give this pair a bashing as we did to the two last year, and then we can be on our way." Said a stocky, bearded scruff with a broken nose to the leader.

"Would that be the two that are standing behind you at this moment?" Bill asked with a smile.

Ginger looked over his shoulder and said, "Yes, that would be them."

Standing quietly behind the gang was Ron leaning on a long metal bar from his smithy and Bert, who was resting on his broad shoulders the oak pole with a hook on the end that he used to open the high windows in the bar.

Looking at the leader, Bill said, "It's your move, I think, but knowing Bert and Ron there, it would have been a close run thing last year, and if I were a betting man, I would say that was where your friend here got his broken nose.

That was when there were six of you against the two of them, so how do you rate your chances now that it will be six of you against the four of us?"

As the reverend finished speaking, the bearded biker, thinking that the vicar would be the easiest target, pulled a flick knife from his pocket and, lowering his head, rushed straight at him.

Unfortunately for him, Bill had fought bigger and more vicious opponents than this in Holland, and as soon as he came within range, Bill calmly lifted the broom handle and drove it into the biker's groin.

Letting out a high-pitched squeal, the thug fell to the ground writhing, releasing the knife upon his impact with the road.

"Oops, how careless of me; this broom handle appears to have a mind of its own." Said Bill, retrieving the knife from the road before turning to the leader without giving a second glance at the whimpering thug lying in the road grasping his crotch, "The odds seem to be getting better and better in our favour, don't you think, so do you want to reconsider finding those licences?"

Turning to Dave Gregory, he said, "Are you happy with that, or do you want to take them to the police house and deal with all that paperwork?"

"As long as they can provide me with the relevant documents, I'm satisfied with that arrangement."

Turning to Ron and Bert, Dave Gregory asked,

"Do you gentlemen wish to press charges over the events of last year?"

They shook their heads, and Ron turned to the vicar and said, "May I borrow that knife you picked up for a minute?"

Bill handed the knife to Ron, and while the policeman took note of the bikers' details, he and Bert took turns walking around the bikes, cutting the fuel lines.

The vicar saw that the bikers wanted to object, but Ginger shook his head and said, "How far is it to the nearest garage to repair the fuel lines?"

Ron smiled and declared noncommittally that the local garage was closed, but they could push their bikes to Upper Dipping, only four miles up the hill. Replacing his notebook in his breast pocket after inspecting all of their licences, PC Gregory turned to face the bikers for the final time and said. "Now pick up your friend and be on your way; I also suggest you don't return to Lower Dipping because the welcome may not be so friendly next time."

The sorry-looking bikers collected their friend from where he lay and disappeared, pushing their bikes toward Upper Dipping; PC Gregory turned to Ron, Bert and the vicar and said. "Thank you for your assistance, gentlemen, as that could have turned very nasty, and Bill, why are you carrying that broom handle?"

"Well, it was the only thing I could find in the shop to use as a weapon, and it was cheap."

CHAPTER 8

The Second Letter
Saturday

Bill was in his study working on Sundays sermon and appreciating the quiet, there being no further murders, visits from the police inspector or biker gangs, when the early post arrived with a second letter from Reverend Peters,

Dear Reverend Davis,

I have seen in the Kentish Times that there has been a murder, and Micky Jordan was the victim, and I can honestly say that I'm not surprised or disappointed.
I know this is not a very Christian attitude, but I did not like that boy and his actions.
Inspector Doyle visited me this morning to ask about the letter I sent to you shortly after my departure.
I informed the inspector that the girl Micky had photographed no longer lived in this country as she had emigrated to Australia last month with her parents,

so there was no way they could be responsible for his death.

I would suggest that you leave trying to find Micky's killer to the police as it might prove to be very dangerous for you and anybody helping you if the killer feels threatened.

If I can further assist, please get in touch.

Yours faithfully

David Peters

After reading and pocketing the letter, Bill cleared his head by taking Duchess for a walk in the woods before lunch.

As he and Duchess passed Lower Dipping House while walking through the village, Anne and Archie appeared from the garden gate.

With a cheery wave, Bill said, "I'm off to the woods. Would you care to come with me?"

Looking up with wide eyes, Anne said. "Oh, vicar, you are awful propositioning a poor innocent gal like me." The poor vicar's face turned scarlet, and Anne grinned wickedly. "I'm just teasing." She said, slipping her arm through his, "Mind you, you're not bad looking."

Looking at Anne, he said with a smile. "You're far from ugly yourself," and she gave his arm an affectionate squeeze as she moved a fraction closer.

Setting off in the direction of the woods, arm in

arm, with the dogs leading the way, they chatted about the other members of the dog walkers and Miss Harlan's possible shady past.

Passing the gypsy encampment with its multi-coloured caravans beside the meandering stream, they gave Mrs Lee, who was boiling something in a huge pot over a fire, a friendly wave before entering the woodland with its ancient oaks; and followed the path until they reached the stream where the willows hung over the fast-running water.

Still, arm in arm, they followed the woodland path with its broken beams of sunlight until they spied a faint trail off to the left, leading to a cluster of young saplings beside the stream.

Following the indistinct path, they discovered themselves in a clearing out of sight from the trail. "This looks like the place in the photograph," said Bill, as he stood straddle-legged in the centre of the clearing with the willow branches hanging over the stream as in the photograph and as he turned, he spied amongst the bushes away from the stream, where the rabbits had cropped the grass short.

To Anne's surprise, Bill dropped to his knees on the short grass and pointed at three shallow holes shaped like a triangle.

Looking over his shoulder, Anne laughed and said, "This is like going for a walk with Davy Crockett; now tell me, Mr Crockett, what do you think made those marks?"

"Well, if I were a photographer like Micky, I would say it was a tripod made for holding a camera," Bill replied, getting back to his feet.

Anne shuddered and said, "The more I hear about that Micky Jordan, the less pity I feel."

Upon returning to the vicarage, Bill and Anne walked in the door to the kitchen, still holding hands, to discover Mary and Ron sitting across the kitchen table, similarly holding hands and sharing a pot of tea.

The look of surprise on all four of their faces and the sudden breaking hands of the two couples at the sight of their siblings caused them to burst into laughter suddenly.

When Bill said they had been in the woods, Ron and Mary's eyebrows shot up in surprise.

Seeing their expressions, Bill said. "Oh, for goodness sake, we were looking for clues as to who the two men were in the photograph, and we found some."

Anne nodded in agreement, and they sat down and told their siblings about the hidden clearing and the tripod marks.

"Do you mean to tell me that the two men stood there and allowed Micky to photograph them?" Asked Mary.

"I don't think it was like that," Bill said. "Remember in the letter how Micky convinced the girl he loved her? I'm confident that Micky was one of the men in the burnt photo and had the camera set on a timer.

We also assume that to keep him quiet; he was murdered by the other man in the photograph after he had tried to blackmail him like he did the girl's parents."

"Makes sense to me," said Ron.

Bill took the letter from his pocket for the others to see and said. "I received another letter in the post this morning from David Peters. Saying to forget the girl and her family that he had mentioned in the first letter as they are all now in Australia,"

After reading the letter, Anne said. "I think that Reverend Peters knows more than he is saying with his warning about the killer after reading that."

Mary sat back in her chair and said. "I agree with Anne about the Reverend Peters and think you should show the letter to Inspector Doyle immediately and tell him what you discovered in the woods this morning."

"I'll take the letter down to the police station and give it to Sergeant Wilson to pass on to Inspector Doyle after the Dog Walkers meeting," said Bill, tucking the letter back into his pocket.

CHAPTER 9
The Second Meeting
Saturday

As it was a dry afternoon, they decided to walk up to the Manor. The girls led the way, with Ron and Bill following.

"What's this with the hand holding with my sister?" Asked Ron with a broad grin on his scarred face as the vicar's face reddened again.

"Well, it just sort of happened, and by the way, how long have you been popping around to the vicarage to have tea with my sister?"

It was Ron's turn to turn red as Bill laughed.

"It started not long after you arrived in the village, and Mary came into the garage wondering if I could mend the broken chain on her bike, and then we bumped into each other a couple of times whilst walking the dogs."

"How many times did you have to walk the dog before you could accidentally bump into her on purpose?'

"Quite a few; the poor dog was exhausted. Thankfully, I plucked up the courage to ask Mary out before the dog dropped dead from exhaustion, and it progressed from there."

"Did Anne know?"

"Mary told Anne to give you a nudge because you were too shy to make the first move."

At that point, the girls turned around and started giggling like teenagers.

Bill turned to look at Ron and said. "I didn't stand a chance, did I?"

Ron laughed, "Not a hope in hell."

The chattering group were the last to arrive at the Manor and took their seats around the table alongside their dogs.

"Glad we can all be here after the recent events in the village." Said the Brigadier. "No more dead bodies in the vicarage, I hope, reverend".

"Mercifully no, Brigadier, as I don't think Mary would have appreciated having to rewash the hall floor," Bill answered with a smile.

"I have one piece of news, though; the girl and her family mentioned in the first letter I showed you are no longer in the country. So now we know they couldn't be responsible for Micky's death." He took the latest letter from his pocket for them all to see.

"After reading this letter, I think David Peters knows more than he lets on." Said Bert Love, going along with Anne's earlier suspicions.

"That will be for the police to discover, as I will be delivering the letter to Sergeant Wilson after the meeting," said Bill, tucking the letter back in his pocket.

"I always knew that Micky was a bad one." Said Joe.

"He tried to get Rosie Saunders from Crab Apple Farm to pose for him like the girl in the letter, but she had more sense and told her father.

The next time Micky turned up at the farm, he found himself looking down the barrels of Jack Saunder's shotgun before scuttling back to the village with his tail between his legs after Jack informed him that there are a lot of unfortunate shooting accidents on farms and if he came near his Rosie again there would be another one."

"How on earth do you know this?" Bill asked Joe.

"Jack told me the story over a pint one evening in the Mucky Duck."

"Elsie told me a couple of things she had heard about Micky too." Bert interrupted. "Seemingly, he had been seen going through people's dustbins looking for letters that might provide him with information about the householder."

"How would that help him?" Asked Miss Harlan.

It was Mary's turn to speak up. "During the war, whilst in the SOE, we used to go through known collaborators' rubbish. Once, we found a letter from a panzer officer telling his lover when he would next be in the area and even where they would be parked. We were delighted and radioed the information back to the UK, so when the panzers arrived, a squadron of mosquitos was there to greet them.

Alas, the poor French girl had to look for a new lover."

After the chuckles had died down, Ophelia said in

her plummy voice. "That's all very well in wartime, but what is he likely to find amongst the village rubbish?"

It was Joe's turn to speak again, and he sat up in his seat to lean forward, resting his elbows on the table. "Say there was a letter from your sister inviting you to a weekend house party; then he would know that your house should be empty."

"Aha," said the Brigadier. "But the servants would be here."

Joe gave a smile and said. "We aren't all lucky enough to have servants like you, Brigadier, but for people like me, say I had a win on the football pools, and I had thrown the notification letter in the rubbish. Micky would take it out, read it and then know that I might have some money in the house, so all he had to do was wait for me to go out, say to this meeting and then break in."

"Yes, I understand, but I think that is enough talk about this unfortunate young man, and let us now discuss how we can help raise some money for the community." The Brigadier spluttered.

After they had discussed a few ideas about ways to raise money for some upgrades to the children's play park, the Brigadier said, "There is one other item he would like to raise before closing the meeting, and it involves you, Mr Ross, it concerns the travellers you have camping in your field, there are members of this community who think they are an undesirable element to the area and need to leave."

Joe got to his feet and, leaning upon the table, said, "Those travellers, as you call them, are not travellers but are of proud Romany stock and have been regular visitors to this village for as long as I can remember.

Django Lee and his family are all held in high regard in this village, and they are all exceptionally hard-working folk.

They help on the local farms at harvest time and do odd jobs in the village, sometimes for no charge, particularly for the older folk.

The locals who have lived for generations in this village and not just moved down from London have no problems with the Romanies and consider them as friends. So, in answer to your question, Brigadier, I shall not be telling them to move off my land."

The Brigadier stood stunned at being spoken to in this way, called the meeting to a close, said he had some important phone calls to make and left the room closely followed by Ophelia, whom they heard remark to her husband in hushed tones. "That frightful little oik will have to go."

Joe gave a satisfied grin, and the rest of them, stunned by the Brigadier's sudden departure, set off toward the village.

"Well, it seems there will be no free drinks in the library this week," Ron said. "Looks like we're off to your place, Bert."

"Certainly, just don't expect free drinks." Answered Bert with a smile.

"I don't think the Brigadier appreciated your remark about the servants and the Lees'," Ron said to Joe as they all made their way down to the village.

"Sometimes the Brigadier gets right up my nose with his hoity-toity attitude. So I got a dig in to bring him down to earth."

Walking between Anne and Mary, Bill suddenly remembered the letter in his pocket and said.

"Hold on; I must take this letter to Sergeant Wilson. I'll see you in the pub later."

"I'll come with you," Anne said, breaking away from the leading group.

"That will set the tongues wagging in the village,"

"Do you care?" Asked Anne.

"Not a jot," he replied, taking Anne by the hand, set off toward the police house whilst the others made their way to the pub.

As they passed Ron's garage, Bill leaned forward to kiss Anne, stumbled and clumsily buried his nose in her ear. Anne laughed and said, "Was that you trying to kiss me?"

"That was my intention, but I made an arse of it."

"You did rather, but I'll say one thing: you seem to be quickly getting over your shyness." Giving him a come-hither smile.

"I'm being led astray by this wanton doctor; I have got to know."

"Now let's get to the police house and give Sergeant Wilson your letter so we can get on with your practising."

It took a considerable amount of hammering upon the door to the police house before Sergeant Wilson came to the door in his shirtsleeves and no tie.

When he saw who was making all the noise, his face lost its scowl, and he managed a welcoming smile before saying. "Reverend, Doctor, how may I be of assistance?" Whilst opening the door wider as an invitation to enter.

They declined his offer, and Bill reached into his pocket for the letter and handed it to the sergeant. "This is for Inspector Doyle as I thought he might find it of interest as we are of the impression that the Reverend David Peters may know more than he is saying in the letter."

"I'm certain that the recent events with Micky and his mother are unfortunate accidents." The sergeant said, whilst stuffing the letter into his trouser pocket.

"After you have read the letter, maybe you will think differently, and please make certain that you inform the inspector as soon as possible." Said Bill through clenched teeth as he took Anne's hand and left this incompetent member of the local constabulary standing open-mouthed in his doorway.

They arrived at the Mucky Duck, going red in the face upon seeing the knowing looks from the others seated around the tables.

"How did you get on?" Asked Ron.

"That's none of your business." Answered Bill,

going even redder in the face.

Ron laughed, "I meant with the sergeant, not my sister.

"The man is a buffoon." Bill spluttered and told the members of the 'Dog Walkers Society' about the sergeant's belief that the two deaths were nothing but accidents.

"That PC Day and the Sergeant are two of a kind and just waiting for their pensions." Said Joe. "They sat here during the war with nothing to do except sound the air raid siren and arrest the occasional drunk from the anti-aircraft battery on the other side of the woods. Now, they have a real crime; they are all at sea. The only one with any gumption is the young lad PC Gregory, who is still learning."

"That's true," Bill added, "He was as cool as a cucumber when dealing with that motorcycle gang."

"Are you suggesting, Joe, that we must solve the crimes ourselves?" Said Bert.

"Hold on a minute, remember what my letter said. It could become hazardous for anybody asking questions in the village."

"Ooh, we could then call ourselves 'The West Kent Dog Walkers Society/Crime Solvers." Announced Miss Harlan.

"Yes, and you could be Lower Dippings' answer to Miss Marble," called Elsie from the bar from where she had been listening.

When the laughter had ceased, Miss Harlan

snorted a loud "Harrumph," followed by. "If you are going to comment, please try and get the name right; it is Miss Marple."

Elsie chuckled, knowing full well the lady detective's correct name and went back to polishing the glasses.

"What do you say that you and I borrow Anne's car and pop over to Eynsford on Monday and chat with your predecessor to see what he knows about the happenings in this village." Suggested Ron.

"I beg your pardon?" Said Anne.

"What makes you think you can swan off in my car, leaving Mary and me behind?"

"Quite right, Anne, you tell them, and besides, I believe the Pied Bull in Farningham makes an excellent lunch on the way." Said Mary.

Bert and Joe laughed, and Miss Harlan said. "I wish Anne had a bigger car, and I could come too."

Joe piped up and said. "I just happen to." When Ron and Bill interrupted simultaneously with, "Shut up, Joe."

"I'm hurt; it doesn't look like they want me along on the ride, Mr Ross." Said a smiling Miss Harlan.

"What about your patients?" Ron asked Anne.

"There is nothing that won't wait until I get back."

"Looks like we are going to have some company." Said Ron, taking a swig of his beer.

CHAPTER 10

A Day Out
Monday

Eleven o clock Monday morning found Mary, Anne, Ron, and Bill piled into Anne's black Hillman Minx on their way to Eynsford.

Having grown up in Soham outside Ely in Cambridgeshire with its flat fenland, Bill and Mary still found, even after years of living in the Kent countryside with its orchards and hop gardens and the gently rolling hills, so very different.

Cambridgeshire is not unpleasant, with the River Great Ouse meandering across the flat landscape between the small villages and market towns, with the horizon broken only by the odd windmill and church spire.

After a half hour's drive, they approached the ford at the village of Eynsford.

"Did you know that Eynsford gets its name from Saxon times and was known as Aegen's ford? Whomever Aegen was." Said Mary from her place in the front seat next to Ron.

"You've been taking history lessons from Miss Harlan, haven't you?" Bill asked.

"Bill, do you know where David Peters lives in the village?" Asked Ron over his shoulder.

"He told me before he left that he had bought a cottage three houses past the Plough public house, and if I am not mistaken, that is the Plough just over the river," Bill said, pointing at the pub sign.

Ron said. "What's it to be, the bridge or the ford?"

Bill quickly answered. "It has to be the ford."

Ron put his foot down hard on the accelerator, and they shot towards the water with Anne screaming, "No, the water will come in through the holes in the floor."

But it was too late as the Hillman hit the water with an almighty splash, and as Anne had foretold, the water flowed into the car, and the engine died as the water hit the electrics.

"You dozy bugger, you great hulking oaf you, you, you've killed my car." Screamed Anne into her brother's ear whilst hitting him about the head and shoulders.

Once they had gotten over the shock of the sudden stop, Mary and Bill were helpless with laughter at the siblings' antics.

Whilst draped over the steering wheel and incapable of laughter, Ron said between bouts of giggling like a girl. "Stop hitting me, and don't worry, once I get the engine dried out, your precious car will start again; now again, please stop hitting me."

Anne then turned on Bill. "What do you find so funny?"

"Nothing, nothing at all; what Ron has done to your car is terrible."

"You creep," said Ron. You don't half tell a lot of porkies for a vicar."

Anne finally calmed down and saw the funny side of events and said. "Well, if you two strapping men think that us girls are wading through the water to get to dry land, you have another thing coming. You are going to have to carry us."

Bill thought about saying that nine inches of water would hardly be classed as wading but thought better of it.

Climbing from the car and standing in the cold water of the River Darent, Bill helped Anne from the back seat and lifted her into his arms with her arms around his neck.

After he had taken a couple of paces, he stopped and said. "You know how clumsy I am; after Saturday night, I may stumble and drop you into the river if I don't get a kiss."

Looking into his eyes, Anne said. "That is the most unvicar-like behaviour I have ever heard of."

"It must be the company I have been keeping recently, and besides, I'm not certain if there is such a word as unvicar."

"There is now," she said, paying her dues before reaching dry land.

As the men deposited the girls on the dry road beside the ford, a scruffy grey-bearded man came in their direction from The Plough public house.

"You folks look like you need a hand getting out of

the river?"

"You could say that, and I don't suppose you have any ideas?" Asked Ron, looking down at the man from his six and a half feet.

The man gave a gap-toothed grin and said, "I'm known locally as 'Tractor Tom', and I bet you can guess why."

"You have a tractor and earn a few bob pulling stranded cars from the river."

"Correct," said Tom. "Every year, some daft buggers try to drive at top speed through the ford and get stuck. Not that I'm calling you a daft bugger." Said Tom, taking in Ron's bulk.

"I would," said Anne.

"And how much will this Christian act of kindness cost me?" Asked Ron.

"Ten bob." Replied Tom.

"Ten bob?" Roared Ron, "This man is a bigger rogue than Joe Ross."

Tom looked up sharply. "You know Joe Ross from Lower Dipping?"

"Yes," said Mary. "We're from Lower Dipping, and he's our friend. We were only having a drink with him the other day."

"That being the case, I should charge you double."

Upon seeing Mary's face fall, he said, "Just teasing you, Miss. Joe and I are good pals; now you all wait here while I go and get my tractor, and then you can buy me a pint."

Half an hour later, Ron had got the Hillman's engine dried and running whilst Bill had mopped out the inside as much as possible with some cloths supplied by Tom at no extra charge, and they were all sitting around a table in the Plough.

Tom had put his rusty old Ferguson tractor back in its shed, ready for the next speeding tourist and was on his third pint at Rons' expense when he said. "What's brought you to Eynsford? A day out with the young ladies."

"You could say that. I'm the vicar at Saint Marys in Lower Dipping and have come to see my predecessor, David Peters, who lives here in Eynsford."

At the mention of David's name, Bill saw Tom's face fall as he said. "I'm sorry to tell you this, but your friend appears to have had an accident last night, and Mrs Osbourne, his housekeeper, found him lying at the foot of his stairs this morning."

"Is he still alive?" Bill asked Tom.

"Sort of." He said. "But he was still unconscious when they took him to Dartford Hospital in the ambulance."

We all looked at each other, and everyone except Tom thought of the similarity between this supposed accident and the killing of Micky Jordan.

"What is it?" Asked Tom when he saw the looks on our faces.

Bill explained about the murders in Lower Dipping and how the killer had set them up to look like accidents.

"But why would anyone want to attack poor old Reverend Peters here in Eynsford? The poor old boy wasn't doing anybody any harm here." Said Tom.

"No, but he sent Bill a couple of letters," said Ron.

"The first letter told him to beware of Micky Jordan, who was to become the first murder victim, and the second letter warned him that he could be in danger if he tried to investigate the murders himself.

After reading the second letter, we thought he knew more than he was saying.

We decided to come to Eynsford to ask Reverend Peters in person what further information he could tell us, but now we are here, you tell us that he has had a fortunate accident similar to the one that killed Micky Jordan."

"Well, I never." Said Tom, draining his pint. "The least I can do is show you where he lives," and he got to his feet.

They all got up from the table, with Tom leading the way out when he suddenly jumped back onto the porch, nearly knocking into Mary, muttering, "Rozzers. The police and I don't always see eye to eye, so if you don't mind I will make myself scarce and wish you all the best of luck in your search," as he disappeared out through the back door of the pub.

Slightly stunned by this sudden departure of their saviour, they made their way out onto the road to be confronted by the sight of Inspector Doyle and Sergeant Cornwell hammering on the door of the nearby cottage.

Upon seeing the group, the Inspector turned in their direction and said. "What are you all doing here?" In an aggressive tone.

"Much the same as you, I assume," Bill replied. "We came to visit David Peters but got here too late."

"What do you mean, too late?" He snapped.

"Seemingly, he had an accident similar to Micky Jordan, but the reverend isn't dead, though he is unconscious."

We might have seen him earlier if we had received the second letter sooner.

Surprised at this, Bill asked the Inspector. "Err, when did you receive the letter?"

"We received it this morning, of course."

"In that case, if I were you, I would have a word with Sergeant Wilson in Lower Dipping as I gave him the letter on Saturday evening, and if he says otherwise, Doctor Clements was with me when I handed it over. Oh, and by the way, to save you the trouble of asking around about the whereabouts of Reverend Peters, he was taken to Dartford Hospital by ambulance this morning.

Now, if that will be all, Inspector, we will be on our way as we have two hungry young ladies to whom we have promised lunch."

With that, they left the two bemused police officers standing at the retired reverend's front door and returned to the car before heading toward Farningham.

Ron said as he couldn't withstand another battering from Anne, he would have to use the bridge, though it wouldn't be as much fun as the ford.

After a most enjoyable lunch, they took a leisurely drive back to Lower Dipping, discussing what they would do next about Micky's murder. They concluded that there was very little they could do until David Peters came out of his coma.

Upon their return, Bill and Anne spent a lazy afternoon full of steak pie sprawled on the vicarage sofa until it was time for Bill to take Evensong for his twenty parishioners, after which he decided to nip down to the Mucky Duck for a quick pint.

All of the Dog Walkers Society except for the Brigadier and Ophelia were seated around the table in the Saloon Bar and turned to face Bill as he entered the bar and said, "Hello, are we having a meeting?"

"Sort of." Said Bert. "Joe has received a letter today from the Brigadier who has expelled him from the group for inappropriate behaviour."

Bill was shocked by this presumptuous behaviour by the Brigadier and said. "He surely doesn't have the right to expel anyone from the group without the backing of the others?"

"He most certainly does not." Said an indignant Miss Harlan.

"I know the Brigadier instigated the first meeting, but we did not vote him chairman.

"This sounds like something that Ophelia would come up with. We all heard what she said at the end of the last meeting." Said Anne.

The irritation showed in the vicar's tone as he ordered his pint. "I'll go and have a word with the Brigadier in the morning and see what he has to say,"

"Have you heard how the old reverend is fairing?" Asked Ron.

"I rang the hospital this evening before coming here, and they answered that he was comfortable but had not yet regained consciousness."

"I heard from my old mate Tom that you were trying to walk on water today." Said Joe.

"Ha, ha," Bill replied. "It's a pity we don't have a ford here, and then you could have a similar rescue service and make a few quid."

"Who do you think sold him the tractor?" Answered Joe.

"How does that not surprise me," Bill said, giving up on trying to get one over on the tricky rogue.

CHAPTER 11

Back to the Manor
Tuesday

On Tuesday morning, Bill has the first of his three weekly home visits to a couple of the village's elderly parishioners.

The first is Mrs Johnson, who moved to the village after her husband was killed in the fourteen eighteen War and lived in a pretty cottage opposite the Mucky Duck.

He knocked on her front door and entered shouting, "It's only me, Mrs Johnson, Bill Davis, and I've got Duchess with me."

A faint voice came from the lounge, "Come in, vicar and bring that beautiful girl with you."

Entering the lounge, Duchess headed across the room to the frail white-haired woman in her armchair beside the window and laid her head in the older woman's lap.

"Oh, Duchess, you are a beautiful girl, but it appears you now have some competition in the form of an auburn-haired doctor." Mrs Johnson said whilst stroking the top of the dog's head.

"Flora, I don't know what you are talking about.

Doctor Clements and I are just friends."

"Yes," she said. "Friends joined at the lips last night outside the pub."

"Enough of my private life," He said, wishing his red face would subside. "What's the idea of leaving your front door open; anyone could come in, and then what would you do?"

Still grinning at his red face, she answered his question by pulling a commando knife from beside her cushion.

Forgetting that he was a vicar, he exclaimed, "Where in God's grace did you get that?"

"My nephew gave it to me; he was in the commandos during the War. Besides, I normally used to lock the door to keep that nasty little bugger Micky Jordan from coming in. But now that he's dead, I don't feel the need."

"Did he ever try to get in?" Bill asked.

"He came in once without being invited, but he didn't notice my nephew was in the kitchen making a pot of tea and heard Micky asking me for money.

You should have seen the look on his face when my nephew came out of the kitchen. His face went from green to red to white as he tried to run.

It was so funny to watch. Little Jimmy caught him by the scruff of the neck and threw him so hard out of the door that he didn't stop bouncing until he hit the pub wall across the road.

I shouldn't say this to a vicar, but I nearly wet myself with laughter. It was a grand sight to see, I'll tell you."

Bill picked up a photograph from the mantlepiece of a soldier who towered over Mrs Johnson by a good eighteen inches and said. "Is this your little Jimmy?"

"Yes, that's my wee Jimmy; he's about the same size as your lady friend's brother."

"Did Micky ever try to come back?"

"No, he never tried to come in here, though whether he tried any of the other old folk in the village, I couldn't say."

"Did you see Micky again after that day?"

"Not to talk to, it was the coronation day, and I was in the school hall when the party was on.

What a good do that was with all the singing and dancing. I got squiffy with one too many gins. I was talking to Joe Ross when I saw Micky sticking his head around the door.

I thought at first he might have been looking for his mother, but she was busy trying to get that nice Brigadier and his wife to get up and dance, and when I looked again, he was gone."

Bill spent another twenty minutes chatting to Flora before he and Duchess said farewell and headed to visit Jack Cooper, the next pensioner on his list.

Jack lived in the middle of a run of cottages opposite the school with his wife, May.

Like Flora, he spends much of his time looking out the window at all the comings and goings in the village due to his lack of mobility.

Before he could lift the lion's head, brass door knocker May answered the door.

"Saw you coming, vicar, so I thought I would beat you to the door and say hello to you too, Duchess." Said the small grey-haired woman with skin that many a younger woman would envy.

As Duchess and Bill entered the cottage, a deep voice came from the sitting room. "Come on in, Bill and take a seat. May get Bill a glass of my homemade bitter, or maybe he would prefer a glass of last year's elderflower."

"A glass of elderflower would be very refreshing for a change," He said whilst shaking hands with the large man before taking his seat.

Jack is a retired farm labourer renowned in the parish for his excellent home brews of both beer and wines.

When he was younger, he was an excellent gardener, often winning first prize for his vegetables in the local shows.

"First time I've seen you since the coronation, and it appears you've had a bit of excitement with that Micky Jordan being found dead in your vicarage."

"That's not the only excitement he's been having either." Said May as she brought in my glass of wine.

"Oh, what else has he been up to," asked Jack innocently.

"He's seeing that nice lady doctor."

"Aw, she's a bit of all right. Is that Doctor Clements," Jack chuckled.

Bill shook his head as he felt his face starting to turn red again and took a sip of his wine. Then, to change the subject, he said, "Enough about me. Is there anything I can help you with?"

May said, "No, vicar, we are getting along fine. Our daughter Joan pops in twice weekly with groceries and sometimes brings the little ones. "What a handful they are."

"Joan offered to take us to the school for the coronation party, but I was a bit tired after my trip to the hall to watch that television contraption you arranged for us." Said Jack.

As May turned towards Bill and said, "It was grand to see, but I don't see it catching on though; it will never replace the wireless. So we were glad to get home, and Jack got comfy in his chair by the window whilst I made us both a nice cup of tea.

"Yes," said Jack, "it was while I was looking out the window that I saw that little weasel Micky Jordan hanging about at the school. Not that Micky stayed long at the school before starting up the road with his uncle."

Shocked at this news, Bill said, "I didn't know Micky had an uncle in the village."

"Yes, that useless great lump, Humphrey Wilson, the police sergeant, is or should I say was Kathy Jordans, half brother and brought Kathy and Micky to the village where he got them the prefab after the War.

That was the worst thing that ever happened to this village. No sooner had Kathy and Micky arrived than things started to go missing from people's houses, and the property was damaged.

When people complained to Wilson, he just kept saying that it was youthful high spirits or there was no proof Micky had done anything wrong."

"Who else in the village knew Sergeant Wilson was Micky's uncle?" Bill asked.

"Surprisingly, not that many. There was the Brigadier because he became a magistrate a couple of years after the War, and it got so bad that some people complained about Micky to Sir Hector, who mentioned it to his wife, and that was how we found out."

"How was it that you found out?"

"May used to do a bit of cleaning up at the Manor for the Brigadier's wife, and one day, she overheard the sergeant telling Sir Hector that as Micky was his nephew, maybe the Brigadier could leave him to deal with all disciplining."

"Thanks for the information, Jack; that's cleared up a few questions I had, and also, thanks for the wine; it was delicious."

As Bill left, he called Duchess, who came from the kitchen carrying a large beef bone.

He called out and thanked May for the wine before saying to one delighted dog, "I hope you said thank you too."

After dropping a contented Duchess off at the vicarage with her bone, Bill headed up to the Manor to try and sort out the nonsense of the letter the Brigadier had sent to Joe.

Hopkins, the Brigadier's dark-haired manservant, answered the door

Taking a backward pace, he said. "Good afternoon, sir; please come to the study whilst I inform the Brigadier you are here."

Crossing the entrance hall with its suit of armour standing alongside the large brass dinner gong on its wooden frame, Bill came to the open study door. Entering the Brigadier's inner sanctum, a room he had never been in before, he was impressed by all of the Brigadier's memorabilia scattered around the room.

Along with an SS dagger on his desk, there was a Zulu shield complete with assegai and several other pieces of tribal art, which he assumed the Brigadier had gathered from his time in Africa.

From India, there was a figurine of the many armed goddess Kali sitting alongside the fire and a jezail musket with its overly long barrel hanging on the wall above the mantle. The one thing that did surprise him was a pair of crossbows with two quivers of bolts sitting in a corner.

As Bill bent over to look at the crossbows more closely, he heard the door open, and the Brigadier entered the room.

"What ho, vicar, and what can I do for you?"

Bill stood up, looked directly at the Brigadier and said, "It's all a bit embarrassing, Brigadier."

The Brigadier interrupted him and said." Don't tell me. It's about the letter I sent to Joe Ross expelling him from the Society; I now consider it a huge mistake.

I sent that letter after a few gins and was still annoyed at his comments about my servants and our disagreement over the gypsys'.

In hindsight, my comments may have sounded a bit pompous."

"It was more than a bit pompous, Sir Hector; it was extremely condescending and gave the impression you considered yourself superior to the rest of the group."

"Oh, my dear man, I never intended to give that impression to the group." Said the shocked Sir Hector.

"Vicar, I would appreciate it if you would convey my apologies to the others and an invitation to come to the Manor on Saturday, where I will apologise in person."

The Brigadier said, "Thank God, sorry, vicar, I mean, thank goodness I have got that off my chest; it's been worrying me all day what I was going to say, and now that I have what would you like to drink?"

Bill, seated in a sizeable over-stuffed armchair with a brandy, looked around the room. "I was admiring your mementoes before you came in and was surprised by the crossbows amongst the modern weapons."

"The crossbows aren't mine; they belong to Ophelia; while we were in India in the thirties, there was a terrorist bomb attack on Government House in which Ophelia's hearing was damaged by the explosion, leaving her unable to withstand loud noises. The doctors call the problem hyperacusis.

Ophelia and I used to go hunting in the bush, but after the explosion, Ophelia couldn't withstand any loud noises, so a firearm was out of the question.

I asked the regimental doctor if there was any way around the problem, and he came up with the answer of crossbows.

I showed a sketch of what I required to a local craftsman, and he made those two crossbows you see sitting in the corner.

Eventually, Ophelia became very proficient in their use, better than me, to be honest."

After spending a pleasant afternoon chatting with the Brigadier, the vicar returned to the vicarage in time for dinner with Mary, and later in the evening, Anne and Ron came across to the vicarage, where they joined Mary and Bill for a late supper, Bill told them of his earlier conversation with the Brigadier and how Flora Johnson's wee Jimmy had bounced Micky across the road and into the pub wall.

Ron said, "I bet that was a sight; Jimmy's a big lad. I'm surprised that Micky didn't run complaining to the police."

"That's another thing I learned today: that Micky's uncle is Humphrey Wilson."

"Bloody hell!" Exclaimed Ron, "You're getting pretty good at this detecting lark."

"Not really, it's just that people like to talk to a vicar; now, if you don't mind, I find myself needing some medical attention."

"My brother appears to have overcome his shyness," said Mary. "Come on, Ron, I will walk you home. You know how afraid you get in the dark."

CHAPTER 12

Joe's Secret
Wednesday

Wednesday morning, after a phone call to the hospital to check on how David Peters was progressing, only to be told there was no change, Bill decided to take Duchess for a walk as far as Joe's cottage to inform him of how his visit to the Manor had gone.

As he crossed the yard to the cottage, he heard a dog crying from inside the large corrugated iron shed in the corner of the yard.

Duchess dashed across the courtyard and started pawing at the shed door, which caused the crying of the dog in the shed to get louder.

As Bill opened the door to the shed, Joe's dog Rex shot out, almost knocking him over, and Duchess rushed in, whining over Joe's still form that lay beside a pile of packing cases and sporting a deep cut to his head that was pooling blood onto the floor.

Dear God, Bill thought, don't let him be dead and kneeling beside Joe, felt for a pulse in his neck. It took a moment before he felt the faint but slow beat; thankfully, Joe was alive.

Leaving Duchess to look over him, Bill went out to the tap in the yard and splashed some water into an old chamber pot that Joe used to feed the chickens.

Carefully carrying the pot so as not to spill the water into the shed, Bill dipped his handkerchief and bathed the cut on Joe's head.

As he washed away the dried blood, Joe began to stir and tried to sit up.

"Lay still, you daft bugger," Bill said, holding the handkerchief against the wound, which started bleeding again.

They stayed like this a little longer before Bill let Joe sit up.

Looking dazedly around him, Joe said, "I hope that's water in that guzunder?" Looking pointedly at the chamber pot beside him.

"What on earth is a guzunder?" Bill asked, relieved that Joe was more like his old self.

Looking again at the chamber pot, he smiled, "It's a chamber pot and called that because it goes under the bed at night."

"Ha bloody ha, you're obviously feeling better," Bill said, helping him to his feet. "Now let's get you into the house, and I will call Anne because I think that cut needs stitching."

Half carrying Joe across the yard, Joe said, still smiling. "For a vicar, you don't half swear a lot."

"If Saint Peter had parishioners like you, he would be swearing as well," Bill replied, pushing open the cottage door.

Joe's cottage wasn't dirty, but it was untidy and missing that woman's touch.

"I don't know where Rex has disappeared to; he shot out of the shed when I opened the door as if the devil himself was after him," Bill said, sitting Joe down at the table with its patterned oilcloth tablecloth before using Joe's phone to call Anne.

While waiting for Anne, Bill put the kettle on for a pot of tea and asked Joe. "What happened to you in the shed?"

"Not so sure; Rex and I had just returned from our evening stroll through the woods when he suddenly dashed into the shed. Which is surprising as nowadays Rex rarely dashes anywhere."

"He fairly dashed out of the shed when I opened the door. I don't know where he dashed to, though."

"Don't worry about him; he will come home when he's hungry. Now, where was I? Oh yes, I was following the dog into the shed when I caught a slight movement out of the corner of my eye before a packing case hit me.

And just before I passed out, I saw a hand raised holding what looked like a small rolling pin when Rex ran at the attacker before letting out a yelp as the shed door slammed shut."

"I think you should buy your dog a juicy steak when he comes home because I think he just saved your life," said Bill, reaching for the boiling kettle.

As he was pouring the tea, Anne arrived at the cottage door accompanied by a subdued Rex, looking very sorry for himself.

Anne inspected the gash on Joe's scalp before saying, "Would you like me to take you to the hospital, or do you trust me to stitch your wound."

"Get stitching, and I hope you have some aspirin in that bag, as I've got a splitting sore head."

Anne sipped her tea and grimaced as she tied off the last stitch.

"That is terrible tea." She said.

"It's what we called Tommy's tea in the paras; a cup of this would keep you going for hours. Would you like a second cup?" Bill asked with a smile.

Anne shook her head and, after kissing Bill on the cheek, said. "Joe, I will leave you in the vicar's capable hands as I have other patients waiting for me back at the surgery, and if the sore head gets too bad, I've left you a couple of strong painkillers on the table."

Joe gave Anne a nod of thanks as she left, which he immediately regretted as he had forgotten his sore head.

As the sound of Annes Hillman faded, Rex came over and lay his head on Joe's knee.

Joe looked down at his old faithful dog and said. "The Vicar here says I owe you a steak, and I think he's right. I don't have any steak, but would a beef bone do?"

The dog's tail began drum furiously on the floor at the mention of the word bone.

"Bill, would you mind opening the cupboard next to the sink and taking out a bone for my saviour." Asked Joe.

After receiving his bone, Rex disappeared into the yard to enjoy his reward.

While all this was happening, Duchess sat on the fireside rug, watching Rex disappear with his bone.

"Poor Duchess, do you think you also deserve a bone?" Said Joe as he got shakily to his feet.

"Sit down," Bill ordered. "I'll get her a bone."

Taking a second bone from the cupboard, he handed it to Duchess and said. "Now say thank you to Joe."

Duchess crossed the room, dropped the bone, and licked Joe's hand before picking it up again and going out into the yard to join Rex.

Seated at the table opposite Joe, Bill said. "You've lived in this village your whole life, haven't you?"

"Yes, and what is your point?" Replied Joe.

"You must have known the connection between Micky and Sergeant Wilson."

"I do, but how on earth do you know?"

"I've spoken to a few people in the village and pieced a few things together on my own, and on my way here this morning, I thought you were bound to know of any connection between Micky and the Sergeant," Bill said, watching Joe closely for any sign of lying.

"It was Micky, the little shit that he is or should say was, that came to me asking to use my shed to store a few items.

I'm no angel, but I wanted nothing to do with Micky and his dodgy dealings.

The next day he's back, and he has his uncle with him; the two of them told me that if I didn't do as Micky wanted, they would plant a few stolen items in the shed for the Sergeant and one of his Constables to find."

"When was this?"

Joe thought about it and said, "About four months ago, not long before you came here. The funny thing was that they never did do as they threatened. I don't know what stopped them, but I never told anyone about them in case they decided to stitch me up."

Joe sat back in his chair and gave a deep sigh as if he was glad to get it off his chest.

"Do you think Sergeant Wilson gave you the cut on your noggin?"

"No, the shape I saw was much smaller than that great lump."

After all the talking, Joe was starting to look a bit pale again and admitted that his head was pounding, so after taking one of Anne's painkillers, Bill half carried him up to his bedroom and laid him in his bed after removing Joe's shoes.

In the corner of the room beside the wardrobe, Bill found a heavy walking stick that he stood next to the bed and instructed Joe to rap on the floor if he wanted anything, as he would be downstairs.

Returning to the kitchen, Bill washed the cups and

used Joe's phone to call Mary.

After a couple of rings, Mary answered, and Bill told her what had happened and that he would spend the afternoon at Joe's while sleeping. And could she ask Ron to come and sit with him after five o'clock so he could take evensong?

"I'll come and sit with Joe instead of bothering Ron." She said.

"No," He answered swiftly. "If the attacker returns, I would rather it was Ron. But you could always come and keep Ron company."

"Ha," she said. "You just want me out of the house in case Anne comes over."

After hanging up the phone, he raided Joe's larder for lunch and settled in an armchair with a stack of bacon sandwiches and a copy of 'The Adventures of Sherlock Holmes', which he had found on a bookshelf beside the fire.

He worked through the short stories, wishing he had Sherlock's analytical brain to determine what was happening in the village.

Bill checked on Joe after a couple of hours, who he found sleeping soundly, so he decided to stroll around the outbuildings.

He found nothing out of order, and the dogs were still contentedly chewing their bones. He knew they would raise the alarm if anyone tried to sneak in.

At half past four, Ron and Mary arrived, accompanied by Bonny and Tilly, who immediately ran over to join the other dogs.

Bill explained what had happened to Joe, who was now sleeping when a knocking came from up the stairs.

"Sounds like the patient has woken up," Bill said, climbing the stairs, followed by Mary and Ron.

"You have two more visitors to keep you company as I have to go and look into the spiritual needs of my parish," Bill said as Joe tried to sit up in the bed. Ron took one look at Joe lying in his bed and said. "Cor Joe, you look like you have just gone two rounds with Rocky Marciano,"

"Only two?" Answered Joe, "It feels like ten."

Bill descended the stairs and said, "There's a painkiller tablet on the kitchen table if he needs it, and I will come back later with Anne to see how he is." Leaving the cottage, he called Duchess away from her games in the yard and returned to the vicarage to find a black police Rover parked outside.

Under his breath, he muttered a quiet "Bugger." Joe was right; he was starting to swear more.

As Bill approached the front door, the Inspector exited the passenger side of the car and said. "Good evening, Vicar. May I have a word?"

Forcing a smile, he said, "Certainly, Inspector, how may I be of assistance, though I have to take Evensong very shortly."

The Inspector gave an uncharacteristic smile and said, "I was wondering if you could accompany us to the Reverend Peters' house tomorrow."

"Why do you need me?"

"Being in the same line of work, you will know if something looks out of place amongst his notes."

"If you think I may be of some assistance, I will come. Now, if you will excuse me, I have to get to work," and Bill made his way to the church, where he found his tut-tutting parishioners waiting.

Later that evening, Anne and Bill returned to Joe's to find him in the kitchen with Mary and Ron tucking into a plate of toad in the hole.

"You appear to be feeling better?" Said Anne to her patient.

"I am, doctor, thank you. Other than a minor headache, I feel fine." Joe mumbled between mouthfuls of Yorkshire pudding.

Bill told them about his forthcoming trip with the Inspector the following day and how they thought he might be able to help them discover the killer.

Bill said, "I didn't think you would appreciate your attack being mentioned to the Inspector as I thought you might not like him poking around your premises. Oh, and by the way, I have to tell you that after my chat with the Brigadier, you're back in the Dog Walkers Society, and he will apologise to everyone on Saturday for his behaviour.

Joe choked on some sausage and said, "Thank gawd for that. I have enough trouble with my sore head without coppers asking me questions, and thanks for talking to the Brigadier."

"What about tonight? Do you want Ron or myself to stay with you in case your attacker returns?" Bill asked, knowing the answer before it came.

"No, Rex and I will be fine." He replied, got out of his chair, reached behind his old battered sofa, and pulled out an old-fashioned bell-mouthed blunderbuss.

"Bloody hell!" Exclaimed Ron, "No wonder you don't want the police poking around."

"Just make sure you keep the doors and windows locked once we are gone, and remember the killer is not averse to starting the odd fire," Bill said as they picked up their coats and returned up the hill to the vicarage for another late supper.

CHAPTER 13
Day Out With The Inspector
Thursday

Bill had just had time to take Duchess for her morning walk before the black Rover pulled up outside the vicarage.

With a "Good morning" to the two policemen, he climbed into the back seat of the Rover and thought how much more comfortable the rear seat of the Rover was than Anne's Hillman; obviously, the CID liked their comfort.

The Inspector leaned over the back of his seat and said. "I appreciate you helping us with this and wondered if you have heard anything new about the deaths."

"Well, I may be able to help from the little I have heard around the village about Micky's background,"

"Whatever you have heard will be of help because the local boys don't appear to have come up with anything." The Inspector answered.

"I will tell you what I have heard, but I will not give you the names of my sources," Bill informed the Inspector, who nodded.

"I will start with what you do know from reading the two letters.

You know about him photographing the girl and blackmailing the parents? He tried the same with Rosie Saunders from Crab Apple Farm, but she had more sense than the first girl and told her father, Jack Saunders.

The next time Micky turned up at the farm, he found himself confronted by Jack with his shotgun, who informed him that if he came near his daughter again, there could be a nasty shooting accident on the farm.

Other things I discovered about Micky was that he was seen by other locals in the village rummaging through people's dustbins looking for information about the householders, and he was known to go walking into old people's houses demanding money."

'How come no one had reported this to the local police?" Asked the shocked Inspector.

"I'll come to that shortly," Bill replied.

"After Micky's death, I had gone around to Kathy Jordan's house to see if there was any way that I could offer any assistance.

Unfortunately, when I arrived, she was passed out in the armchair after consuming the best part of a bottle of gin.

As I left, I noticed she had been burning some photographs in the grate.

I raked amongst the ashes where I found this." Bill said, holding out the photograph of the feet and handing it to the Inspector.

"You should have given me this earlier." Said an irritated Doyle.

"You could have been more approachable when we first met, and as you can see, there is only a little information on that scrap of photo except for the vegetation.

What we did discover, though, was where Micky took the picture."

"When you say we, who else knows about this photograph?" Asked the Inspector.

"Most of the members of the West Kent Dog Walkers Society, actually," Bill said in a matter-of-fact tone as Sergeant Cornwell laughed.

Taking a deep breath to calm his temper, the Inspector asked. "Okay, where was it taken?"

"Doctor Clements and I found a clearing beside the stream in the woodland on the outskirts of the village."

"How do you know that it is the correct place; surely one clearing looks very much like another," He queried.

"I found marks in the grass where Micky's camera tripod had stood amongst some bushes, and the way the willow hangs down over the stream is the same shape as the one we discovered in the photograph;

The Inspector looked again at the scrap photo and said. "The photograph shows two pairs of what looks like two pairs of men's feet standing toe to toe. So how did these men not see Micky?"

"In the first letter, Micky appeared to be a great seducer in achieving his aims; thus, there is a good chance one of the pairs of feet in the photo belongs to Micky," Bill said confidently.

"If he is in the picture, how did he take the photograph?" asked the Inspector.

"He almost certainly had the camera set on a timer to take the shot," Bill replied.

"Returning to what you said earlier, why didn't the people that Micky robbed go to the police? What is the reason?"

"The main reason is that Sergeant Wilson is Micky's uncle. Kathy Jordan is Wilson's half-sister."

"What!" Exclaimed the Inspector at this piece of information, and even Sergeant Cornwell gave a jerk of the steering wheel.

"Yes, seemingly it was him who brought Kathy and Micky to the village after their house in London was destroyed and got them the prefab after the war.

Not long after their arrival, things started missing in the village and property was damaged. When people began complaining to the Sergeant about Micky, he just said it was youthful high spirits, or there was no proof that it was Micky.

After a while, it got so bad that some villagers complained to the Brigadier, who was then the local magistrate and ordered the Sergeant to come to the Manor to explain Micky's behaviour.

Upon his arrival, the Sergeant had said that as the

boy's uncle, the Brigadier could leave him to do the disciplining, and the Brigadier, being of a kindly persuasion, acceded to the Sergeant's request."

"How on earth did you find out all this information?" asked the Inspector.

"I think David Peters was injured because everybody talks to a vicar, and we may find more of what is going on in the village when we go through his papers.

Twenty minutes later, they arrived in Eynsford to be met at the door to David Peters's house by Mrs Osbourne, the housekeeper.

Mrs Osbourne was a tiny woman almost as wide as she was high who gave the impression from the off that she would be with them at all times, and if we made a mess, there would be hell to pay.

She scowled at the two police officers as they entered the front door of the reverend's house. Still, when Bill introduced himself as her employer's successor in Lower Dipping, he was treated to a smile, a shake of the hand and the offer of tea that he readily accepted.

She showed them through to the reverend's study before making the tea. And the study was a very comfortable room with bookshelves on every wall filled with every kind of tome you could imagine.

There was the latest Agatha Christie, old and new books on theology, and volumes on ancient history; there were even a few Enid Blyton books for children.

"The reverend certainly has a very eclectic taste

in literature," Bill said, turning to the policemen standing next to the large walnut desk with its inkwell shaped like a church font and a leather-edged blotter. In the pen tray lay a Platinum pen and pencil alongside what looked like a long hatpin with a large green stone set upon the top.

Behind the desk chair on a wide bookcase shelf sat two old Remington portable typewriters, one in a green leather case and the other in red, alongside a stack of typing paper.

As they started to go through the desk drawers, Mrs Osbourne, obviously deciding it would be the Christian thing to do, entered with a tray containing three cups of tea and a plate of biscuits. The two policemen and the vicar all thanked her for her kindness when Bill said. "Mrs Osbourne, I see amongst the reverend's books that there are some books for children. Can you explain why?"

The housekeeper laughed and said. "The reverend is a canny man and has been in the clergy for many years, and even though he is retired, he still takes the children's Sunday school here in the village. The children's storybooks are one of his ways to ensure the children come back each week. He reads them one chapter from the story at the end of each Sunday's lesson. If they want to hear what happens next, they must turn up the following week."

The Inspector chuckled, "That's canny, all right."

"Can you tell me if you have seen him writing in a diary?"

"I don't know if it's a diary, but he does have a black ledger in which I have seen him inserting sheets of paper." She replied

Looking about the room, the Inspector asked. "Do you see it here?"

She looked around the room and said, "No, I don't see it anywhere. It normally sits beside the reverend's typewriters."

"Thank you, Mrs Osbourne, you have been very kind, and that will be all for now. We will give you a call when we are ready to leave." Said the Inspector courteously."

After Mrs Osbourne had left the room, the Inspector turned and said. "Right, where's that bloody book?"

"Maybe the attacker took it with them." Said the Sergeant.

"It's possible," the Inspector said. "There was no sign on Monday of the room being searched."

They spent another hour searching the office, even going as far as removing the cushion to a large black leather armchair, but all to no avail.

"I give up," said a frustrated Inspector Doyle. "I'm sorry to have wasted your morning, vicar and thank you for your assistance, but I think it's time to return you to Lower Dipping and for me to speak with Sergeant Wilson about his behaviour."

After thanking Mrs Osbourne for the tea and biscuits, they climbed back into the Rover and headed over the bridge for Lower Dipping.

CHAPTER 14
Where is Sergeant Wilson
Friday

After his trip out with the Inspector, the vicar felt he had severely neglected his parish duties and spent the rest of Thursday and Friday trying to catch up.

Friday morning saw him visiting another couple of his parishioners who were unable to make it to church; the first was Mrs Thompson, who had chronic arthritis and couldn't leave the house without assistance, and the second was Mr Davis, 'No relation' who had sprained his knee whilst playing hopscotch with his granddaughter.

Both had been glad to see Bill and catch up on the village gossip, and both had mentioned what a wrong lot Micky Jordan had been.

After lunch, Bill went to the village shop to see James and Doris Edmands and arrange a day for the baptism of their fourth daughter.

James and the vicar stood at the shop counter with their cups of tea while Doris fed the baby when a sudden motorcycle engine roar echoed through the village.

Going to the door, they saw through the door's window a leather-clad rider come to a stop outside the vicarage.

"Looks like you have a visitor," said James, opening the door, "but I don't think it's one of those from the other day."

As the vicar approached the rider, the leather-clad figure removed its helmet to reveal a young man in his twenties with closely cropped blonde hair and freckled cheeks.

Turning to Bill, he smiled upon seeing the dog collar and said. "Hi, my name is Sam Peters; you must be Bill Davis, the local vicar. David Peters, and your predecessor, is my uncle.

Bill shook his hand and said, "Pleased to meet you, and I'm sorry about what happened to your uncle; now, how may I be of assistance."

When I heard what had happened to my uncle, I came immediately to Eynsford where Mrs Osbourne, his housekeeper, told me that you had been assisting the police in searching my uncle's study, looking for any information to help find who had attacked him.

That is why I have come here to Lower Dipping to speak to you and find out if you have discovered why anyone would want to attack an elderly retired vicar."

After listening to Sam, Bill suggested he follow him to the vicarage for some refreshment, where over a cup of coffee, Bill informed him of the two murders that had taken place in the village, followed by the attacks upon his uncle and Joe.

"The police and I know that your uncle kept notes in a black book because Mrs Osbourne told us so, but we could find no sign of it and assumed the attacker or attackers had taken it with them."

"Did you look in his old desk? Sam said, "I remember Uncle David telling me, as a kid, that the desk had secret drawers and cupboards, but he was not forthcoming about how to open them."

"Are you staying in Eynsford?" Bill asked.

"No, I have to go and see if Uncle David has made any improvements before I head off home to Ipswich to tell my father what I have discovered; if I could leave you my parents' home telephone number, I'd like to know if you could be so kind as to inform us of any further developments.

As Bill was tucking the paper with the phone number into his pocket, he started thinking about the items he had seen in Reverend Peter's study. He wondered why the reverend needed two typewriters and a hatpin on his desk.

It was no good, he decided; he had to see the study again and find a way to open the secret compartments in the desk.

Sitting at his desk, he searched the telephone directory to find the reverend's telephone number to contact Mrs Osbourne to arrange another visit.

It took three attempts before Mrs Osbourne answered, and she said she was getting ready before visiting her sister in Swanley this afternoon. But, if he wanted to see the desk, he was welcome to come around tomorrow morning.

After thanking Mrs Osbourne, he had just put the phone down when Mary excitedly entered the study.

"You'll never guess what?" She said.

"Ron's asked you to marry him?" Bill said, looking up with a smile.

"What! Please don't be so stupid; we've only been going out for a short while. No, I was talking to PC Gregory in the village a short while ago, and he asked me if I had seen Sergeant Wilson as he didn't turn up for work today and appeared to have gone missing."

"Maybe he's trying to keep out of the Inspector's way after I told the Inspector about him being Micky's uncle. I'm sure he will soon turn up like the bad penny he is sooner or later."

That same evening, after having finished his monthly report on the parish for the diocese, he decided to pay a visit to his favourite doctor whom he hadn't seen since the evening of Joe's attack. Then, he would have to use all his charm to convince her that she would like to drive him to Eynsford in the morning, and if that failed, he would try to bribe her with another lunch at the Pied Bull.

CHAPTER 15
The Desk Reveals Its Secrets
Saturday AM

The promise of lunch had succeeded where his charm had failed, and after sharing an enjoyable drive through the narrow lanes of Kent, they had found themselves once more in the picturesque village of Eynsford.

Crossing the bridge alongside the ford, they had seen their saviour from their previous visit standing ankle-deep in the water of the ford, washing his tractor. Anne gave a double toot of the car's horn as they passed, to which Tom had given an exuberant wave of his broom in return.

At the reverend's house, Bill introduced Anne to Mrs Osbourne, who said she remembered Anne from the Women Institute baking contest and had never eaten rock cakes since that day before going to the kitchen to fetch them tea and biscuits.

While Mrs Osbourne was away, Anne inspected the book-laden shelves around the study walls as Bill had done on his previous visit with the Inspector.

Bill began his inspection of the desk with its unique inkwell in his search for its hidden secrets, looking for any buttons, levers or movable knots of wood.

When Anne mentioned the children's books on the shelves, he explained how the retired vicar had used them to ensure the return of the children to his Sunday school classes.

He said, "Anne, I need your analytical brain to help me find a way into this desk." He crawled under the desk, looking for a clue to revealing its secrets.

Anne stood running her hands lightly over the desk, checking every knot and bump in the wood like Bill with the same result. She followed this by opening the lid to the inkwell to reveal its blue glass liner filled with thick black ink.

Removing the glass liner with great care to not spill the ink, she placed it carefully on the desk as she closely inspected the inkwell.

"Bill, stop mucking about under the desk and come and look at this, and besides, do you think an elderly retired gentleman would have a secret switch somewhere that he can't reach easily," she said, making him feel foolish as she switched on the desk lamp to shine its yellow light into the inkwell.

Suitably abashed, Bill scrambled to his feet and peered into the inkwell to see what Anne had discovered, and there it was, a small round hole in its base.

Looking at the inkwell with its hole, Bill had a sudden light bulb moment, and the reason for the long hatpin with the green stone now became evident.

Taking the hat pin from the pen tray, he positioned it over the hole and let it fall until there was a click, and the front edge of the desk fell away to reveal the spine of the missing black book.

"Oh, you are a clever girl." He said to Anne and, wrapping his arms around her, gave her a tremendous kiss on the lips.

"Wow, That is most certainly more un-vicar like behaviour. What would Mrs Osbourne have said if she had just entered the room? Now let's open the book and see what it says."

But before they could open the book, Mrs Osbourne entered the room carrying a tray with two cups of tea and biscuits.

"Thank you, Mrs Osbourne, that is most kind of you, and please get another cup for yourself and join us," Bill said, giving her his most endearing smile whilst Anne made retching signs behind Mrs Osbourne's back.

"Are you sure, vicar? I wouldn't want to intrude."

"Not at all; I would like to hear more about the reverend as I only met him for a few days when I took over his old parish, and as you have known him longer than anyone, you are the best person to ask."

"Well, if you are certain," she said, leaving the room to return carrying her cup of tea before settling herself in the comfortable black leather armchair.

"I'd like to ask when you started working as the

reverend's housekeeper?"

"That would have been in nineteen thirty after the death of my Alf. When the Reverend Peters, had not long been appointed as the vicar to Lower Dipping, heard of my Alf's death, he offered me the job as his housekeeper.

He and Alf had known each other from their time together during the Great War, the First World War, to you young people. Alf was declared unfit for active duty in nineteen fifteen after being gassed and transferred to the intelligence section as the driver and batman to Captain Peters as he was then."

Taking a sip of his tea, Bill asked. "What can you tell us of the reverend's early life?"

"All I know is that when the First World War broke out, he had joined the army as a lieutenant and rose to the rank of Major in the intelligence section because of his ability to speak French and German. In addition to this, he was also an excellent mathematician, which helped him decipher intercepted German codes.

By the end of the war, he had been so affected by what he had seen in the trenches and the suffering of the masses of wounded that he had followed his Father and joined the church so that by leading people through prayer, he may encourage others to a healthier lifestyle and by providing social networks to help the less fortunate."

"Is there much else you can tell me? Such as what interests he had outside of the church." Bill asked.

"He was very good with his hands. He used to repair old watches and clocks for his parishioners, and in fact, he took those two old typewriters sitting over by his desk apart and put them back together.

During the last war, he did some hush-hush work for the government but never spoke about what it was. He would say that he was going away for a few weeks, and upon his return, he would look exhausted."

After finishing their tea, Mrs Osbourne returned the tray of cups to the kitchen whilst Anne and Bill returned to inspect the book.

Laying the book on the desk, Anne turned the flyleaf to reveal a sheet of white paper covered in random typewritten letters and numbers.

"Bugger!" She exclaimed in frustration. "He's written it in code, and we don't know what he uses as the key. Can you see anything else in that compartment?"

Crouching, Bill peered into the hidden recess to no avail.

Giving the book a closer inspection, he said. "The pages appear to be sheets of typing paper glued into place. Why would he want to do that?"

Anne looked from the book to the typewriters and said with a wide grin. "Mrs Osbourne told us that he had taken the typewriters apart and put them back together. So what if he has changed the keys in some way." She reached for a blank sheet of paper, fed it into the red typewriter, and typed the first word from the book, but all she got was gibberish.

"Double bugger." She exclaimed in frustration.

"Try the other machine," Bill said as she fed a sheet into the rollers of the green machine and typed the same word again.

This time it came back spelling Saturday.

Bill returned to the red typewriter and typed in Saturday, which came out as the same word in the book.

"Oh, the Reverend Peters is a very clever man." He said. "One typewriter to type the coded message and one to decipher the same message."

After knocking the secret compartment cover back into place, Bill had one last look at the desk, and, for no reason, his attention was drawn to the blotting paper.

He lifted the top sheet of the blotter to discover another typewritten coded sheet, which he carefully removed and placed in the black book before picking up the two typewriters.

"Come on, we had better get these back to Lower Dipping, and the others can help us decipher the code."

After informing Mrs Osbourne that her reverend would soon wake up, they promised to pass his book and typewriters on to the police immediately. And giving her a farewell wave, set off for another lunch at the Pied Bull.

They were seated at their table in the restaurant window after their steak and kidney pie lunch, discussing the recent events in the village.

"What do you think has suddenly brought all this violence to a head; there has to be something that brought it about."

Said Anne.

"I've no idea; nothing new has happened recently except the coronation and the first meeting of the Dog Walkers, but as you said before, maybe Reverend Peters has all the answers, and we will just have to wait for him to wake up unless the answer is in the ledger. Now I will pay the bill, and we can get on our way.

CHAPTER 16

Panic in the Village
Saturday PM

After arriving in Lower Dipping after another delicious steak and kidney pie lunch at the Pied Bull, they were surprised to see the police Inspector's car and a police van parked outside the police house with unknown police officers walking the street.

"What on earth can have happened in the short time we've been away?" Bill said to Anne as they came to a stop outside the vicarage.

Grabbing the Reverend Peter's coded diary and typewriters from the rear seat, they hurriedly made their way up the path to the vicarage. As they approached the front door, it flew open, and the anxious faces of Mary and Ron confronted them.

Mary ran at Bill, threw her arms around his neck, and sobbed into his ear. "You're safe. We wondered what had happened to you."

"I told you last night we were off to Eynsford," Bill said.

"No, you didn't." She replied.

Thinking about the previous night, he realised

that he had been so keen to see Anne he hadn't told Mary of his plans.

"No, I didn't, did I? I'm so sorry, old girl, for worrying you, but what is happening in the village with all these police knocking on people's doors?" Asked Bill.

"Come in, and we'll update you on what you've missed." Said Ron, placing a protective arm around his sister's shoulders and leading the way down the hallway to the kitchen.

Taking a sip of his coffee at the table, Ron told his shocked audience how Miss Harlan had arrived at his workshop in the garage in a state of near collapse.

After sitting her down with a cup of sweet tea, she told him she had been walking Albie in the woods beside the stream when the dog had suddenly shot into the trees, barking furiously. Usually, he was an excellent answering dog, but he refused to return on this occasion and just kept barking.

As Albie gave no sign of returning, Miss Harlan had no option but to follow the sound of his raucous bark through the trees and to discover what had caught his attention.

When she arrived in the clearing, she soon wished she had stayed on the path, for on the far side of the clearing, shackled to a tree by his handcuffs, and with his belt buckled around the tree and in his mouth so that he wouldn't be able to scream was the dead naked body of Sergeant Wilson.

From his wounds, it had been evident that he

had suffered severe torture at his assailants' hands before being castrated and left to die.

Trying hard not to faint at the sight of the dead Sergeant, Miss Harlan had grabbed Albie by his collar and, dragging the straining dog, made her way to Ron's workshop.

Trying hard not to faint at the sight of the dead Sergeant, she grabbed Albie by his collar and, dragging the straining dog, made her way to Ron's workshop.

Leaving Miss Harlan at his workbench with her sweet tea, Ron had run to the police house to inform PC Gregory of Miss Harlan's gruesome discovery.

"Oh, poor Joan, I had better see if there is anything I can do." Said Anne, gathering up her black bag.

"Who's Joan?" Bill queried, "Do you mean Jack and May Coopers' daughter?"

'Who's Joan." Anne Snapped. "No, I do not mean Jack and May Coopers' daughter. You've lived in this village three months, and you don't know that Miss Harlan's Christian name is Joan; sometimes, I despair of you."

And she stormed from the kitchen, followed by Bill's tutting sister.

He looked at a grinning Ron and said. "How was I to know what her first name was?"

Ron gathered up the dirty cups and said. "I didn't know her name was Joan either, and I've lived in this village a lot longer than you. But unlike you, I know when to keep my mouth shut. What kind of sick bastard do you think would do that? I can't say I liked the man, but I wouldn't wish that on anyone."

"Someone with a very sick mind full of hate, and I hope I never meet them without a gun in my hand." Said Bill as he left the reverend's typewriters and coded book in Ron's capable hands whilst setting off around the village checking on his elderly parishioners to ensure that all was well with all the police comings and goings.

Not that he should have worried, as his pensioners were a tough bunch of old folk, and if anything, they were treating it as a great source of entertainment.

Flora Johnson still looked as though butter wouldn't melt in her mouth as she sat with her commando knife tucked under the shawl that covered her legs. She told him to go and find someone that needed comfort.

When he arrived, Jack and May Cooper were still sitting at their sitting room window, watching all the excitement outside whilst drinking their homemade wine.

"Afternoon Bill; come in and sit and enjoy the entertainment. Would you like to try a glass of the pea pod wine?" Said Jack without taking his eyes off the street.

"No thanks, Jack; after I heard of what had happened to the Sergeant, I thought I'd pop in to see if you were both okay."

"I know, it's a terrible thing that's happened," May

said.

"Ha, the Sergeant and his nephew got what they deserved if you ask me." Jack snorted. "They had no friends in the village. No, that's not strictly true; I did see the Sergeant hanging around with that manservant from up at the Manor; Hopkins or Hoskins is his name, I think."

"His name is Hopkins," Bill said. "And I didn't know he was pally with the Sergeant.

But as you both don't appear to be concerned by what's going on in the village, I may as well continue my rounds."

They were so busy staring at the street that they didn't even look in his direction as he left. By four o'clock, he had finished his rounds and returned to the vicarage, where he found Inspector Doyle and PC Gregory seated at his kitchen table, drinking tea with Mary and Ron.

"Ah, good afternoon, vicar; I hope you don't mind us drinking your tea?" Said the Inspector, leaning back in his chair.

Bill smiled a greeting, "Not at all, Inspector, as long as you haven't found the Scotch."

He smiled and said, "I spoke to Doctor Clements briefly, and she informed me that the two of you had made some progress in Eynsford."

"Yes, we discovered a secret compartment in the reverend's desk containing the book Mrs Osbourne had alluded to during our visit."

"Excellent. Do you have it here?" Asked the Inspector eagerly.

Bill returned from his study with the book, some blank paper and the green typewriter.

The Inspector gave him a puzzled look as he deposited his load onto the kitchen table.

Anne entered the kitchen and said, "Ah, inspector, he's showing you our spoils from this morning, I see."

"I see, but I don't understand; why the typewriter?"

"First, we have the book," Bill said, handing it to the Inspector.

He opened the book and exclaimed. "All I see are collections of numbers and letters."

"Yes," Said Anne, "but you don't know that the Reverend Peters was a code breaker for the government during the war."

"So he has written the ledger in code." Said Constable Gregory.

"Correct," said Anne.

"Then how do we make sense of what's written?" Said the puzzled Inspector Doyle.

"That is where this green typewriter comes into use," Bill said with a broad grin as he fed a sheet of paper into the typewriter's rollers, typed the first group of letters from the book, and got the word Saturday as before.

He then returned to his study and, with the red typewriter, typed in the word Saturday and got the same as in the ledger.

"We knew the reverend had a canny brain, but this is nothing short of brilliant." Said the Inspector in awe.

"At the moment, I've got enough on my plate with the murder of Sergeant Wilson, so It would be appreciated if I leave the book with you; maybe you would be able to decipher what the reverend has written?"

"I was hoping you would say that, but first, I had better telephone the Brigadier to tell him I won't be able to attend the Society's meeting this afternoon."

"There's no need." Said Ron, "He called earlier while you were out on your visits to cancel the meeting due to the Sergeant's murder; I also told him that you and Anne had just returned from Eynsford and that I would tell you when you returned that he had called."

"Well, I must be on my way," said the Inspector. "Come along, Constable, we can't sit here all day drinking tea; we must be off, and vicar, I wish you the best of luck in your endeavours."

CHAPTER 17

True Colours
Saturday Evening

After the departure of the two police officers, Bill said to Anne. "Before I begin, Duchess needs a walk. Would you and Archie care to come along?"

"Yes, we could do with stretching our legs.

Ron turned to Mary and said. "It was kind of him to consider us as we've been stuck in the vicarage all day wondering if they were safe and taking his phone messages."

"I'm sorry." Bill said, "I didn't think; please come along."

"I don't think I want to go now." Said Mary.

Ron laughed at Bill's embarrassment, "Don't worry, we're just having you on. Go and enjoy yourselves. I'm certain Mary and I will find some way to keep ourselves entertained while you are gone."

Collecting the dogs, the vicar and the doctor set off hand in hand through the village toward the woods. As they approached the woodland path, Bill felt a familiar prickling sensation on the back of his neck.

It was something you felt in wartime if there was impending danger close by; it was something he had not felt since leaving the paras.

Looking over his shoulder, the only person in sight with their back to him was a man in the phone box. Bill shuddered, and Anne said, "Are you feeling all right? You look worried."

"No, it's just a feeling I have that something is wrong."

As they walked through the woods and deeper into a clearing with its gnarled single oak and slender silver birches, Bill remembered the picture he had seen of the single oak hanging on the walls in Micky's prefab.

Why would he have taken a picture of that particular tree? Admittedly, it was an atmospheric photograph, but was there another reason? It was a large old tree and must have been about four feet across; imagine, it must have been standing in this very spot when William the Conquerer landed at Hastings. Letting go of Anne's hand, Bill started walking around the old tree, looking for a clue as to why Micky had kept its picture on his wall.

On the far side of the tree, away from the entrance to the clearing, and about eight feet from the ground, there was a split in the bark where a branch had broken away, leaving a fissure in the bark and protruding from the gap was something black and shiny.

Stretching up and into the split, Bill touched what felt like a large envelope.

As he was removing it from the hole, Anne came across and asked, "What have you found there?"

"I think this is Micky's secret stash of photos."

Opening the envelope flap, he saw some photographs and negatives filed in smaller envelopes.

The first photograph revealed Micky in a passionate embrace with the owner of the other pair of feet they had in their burnt photo.

"Oh my God," exclaimed Anne, looking over Bill's shoulder, "that's the full picture of the one you rescued from the fire at Micky's house. And that's the Brigadier."

"Shall we try another?" And Anne gave an eager nod of her head.

This one was worse. This time, Micky and the Brigadier were lying naked on the grass of the clearing.

"Oh my God," exclaimed Anne again, "I dread to think what the next one will show."

Taking the third photo from the envelope, Bill turned it over, and this time, he swore. "Bloody hell."

"Oh God, what are they doing now?" Asked Anne.

"It's not them this time," Bill answered.

"How many people was that boy blackmailing?"

"Here are two more," He said, handing over the photograph.

Looking at the picture closely, Anne gave a self-conscious giggle and spluttered. "That's Ophelia, and who's that on top of her?"

"That's not a very good picture of the man's face as all we can see in focus is his bare backside, but I would hazard a guess that it's Hopkins, the Brigadier's manservant."

"Well, he is undoubtedly serving Ophelia, and I'm very impressed as she appears to be very flexible for a woman of her mature years.

Can you work out where Micky took that picture from, as it's an unusual angle?

"It must have been through the dining room window of the Manor, and that will be the dining table around which we had all sat for our meeting.
"

"Is that all there is in the envelope?"

"No, there are pictures of this young lady," Bill said, handing another three photographs to Anne.

"I know her; she left the village with her parents about a year back."

"Do you think this is the girl mentioned in the reverend's first letter?"

She would fit the bill." Said Anne, handing back the pictures.

Bill tucked the envelope containing the photos into the waistband of his trousers before taking Anne by the hand and said. "Let's get out of here and lock this envelope somewhere safe."

Rounding up the dogs, they started to make their way out of the woods when, "Good evening, reverend," came from the cover of trees.

As Bill manoeuvred Anne away from the direction of the voice, he replied. "Evening, Brigadier. It's a wonderful evening for walking the dogs."

"It most certainly is." Said the Brigadier, stepping from the cover of the trees carrying a crossbow.

"I understand that you and the good lady doctor have been to the Reverend Peters's house in Eynsford again in search of the ledger he keeps."

"How do you know of the ledger?" Bill questioned.

The Brigadier paused momentarily when Ophelia's nasal tone called from the shrubbery on the opposite side of the path. "For God's sake, tell him," she said as she stepped into the open.

"Now, my dear, let's avoid blaspheming before the vicar.

If you must know, the Reverend Peters told Sergeant Wilson of his ledger, and he, in turn, relayed that information to me."

"So you were the person that attacked the Reverend Peters," Bill said in disgust.

"Oh no, that was me." Said Ophelia proudly. "The silly little man did not think for one moment that I, a feeble woman, would attack him. Oh, how wrong he was and as soon as he turned his back, I just gave him a tap with my little Yawara stick here and left him at the foot of his stairs as I did with that blackmailing little bastard Micky Jordan."

"You expect me to believe you can disable a full-grown man with that little stick?" Bill asked.

"Oh yes, and she's very good at it too. Show the vicar Ophelia, but not to kill, Yet." Said the Brigadier with a knowing smile.

Ophelia returned her husband's smile and, in a

blink of an eye, took one stride towards Anne, struck her on the side of her left knee with the stick, and stepped back.

Before Anne could react, her leg buckled, and she fell to the ground.

Bill started to turn in her direction when the Brigadier raised the crossbow and said. "Stay where you are; she will be okay in a minute."

Anne shook her head at me and said. "Do as he says, Bill or that mad bastard will shoot."

"Listen to what the doctor says, as we are not ready to kill you yet." Sneered Ophelia.

"So you are going to kill us?" Asks Anne.

"Oh, yes, two bodies will be found in the ashes of the burnt Manor, and you two will fit the bill admirably as we have decided it's time for us to move on."

Bill was amazed at the cold-blooded way they discussed their murders, which gave the impression they had killed many times before.

Trying to give Anne time to recover, Bill kept talking and asked Ophelia. "Did you kill Mrs Jordan and the sergeant as well?"

"Well, yes, that drunken sot enjoyed her drink too much, and as I couldn't be sure of how much of her son's enterprises she knew, she had to go.

She was passed out in the chair when I arrived at her house on coronation evening after leaving the Black Swan, so all it took was a sharp blow to the back of her head with the poker from the fireplace, and there it was job done.

I then knocked over a paraffin heater in a bathroom to give the impression that it was the cause of the fire."

"And the Sergeant?" Bill said, noticing that Anne could now move her leg.

"He was a pleasure to kill, being such a revolting man, and when he thought he could blackmail me into having sex with him, that was the last straw."

"Did you feel nothing for Micky as you appeared very close in the photographs?" Bill said, turning to the Brigadier.

"You have seen the photographs of Micky and myself?"

"Yes, and not only of you and Micky," Bill said, giving Ophelia a knowing look.

"Yes, and he was such a sweet boy," said the Brigadier with a wistful look, but then he got greedy and tried to blackmail me.

"Are you not worried about what the ledger will reveal to the police?" Bill asked whilst trying to position himself closer to the Brigadier.

"I'm not worried as we have already dealt with the problem mentioned in the ledger, and also, as we do not want any written evidence left behind, we have sent Hopkins to deal with it now as we speak. Earlier, he had watched you and the doctor carrying the book and the two typewriters into the vicarage before telephoning the Manor to inform us that you had arrived home. He called again later to tell us you were heading toward the woods.

His next task is to visit your sister and the doctor's

brother to persuade them to hand over the ledger."

"And why would they do that? Bill asked.

"I forgot to mention he will be holding a pistol to your sister's head; now, will you please stand still, or I will have to shoot you before I am ready."

"And what happens after they hand over the ledger."

"Oh, he kills them, of course. He will make it look like the doctor's brother killed your sister and then himself."

"You are insane," piped Anne, "if you think the police will believe that. My brother loves Mary and would never harm her."

Bill saw a slight movement in the shrubbery from the corner of his eye before starting to turn towards Anne, wondering how he was going to protect her from the Brigadier and Ophelia after being shot by the crossbow when the mayhem began.

Ophelia, deciding all this talk had gone on far too long, raised her yawara stick to strike Anne a killing blow when a brown and white snarling dog flew from the shrubbery and grabbed her by the wrist, causing her to let out a piercing scream of pain and drop the stick.

The Brigadier spun towards Ophelia, firing the crossbow bolt as he turned, which pierced the dog's lean chest, causing him to release his grip.

There was a shout of 'bastard' from Joe Ross as he leapt from behind a tree, followed by the explosion of his blunderbuss firing. An even louder scream from Ophelia followed this as she fell writhing to the ground with her hands covering her ears.

Oh my God, Bill thought the blunderbuss blast had triggered Ophelia's hyperacusis.

Bill turned and shoulder-barged the Brigadier to the ground, where he cried in pain from the multiple wounds caused by the shotgun pellets from the blunderbuss.

Bill bent, picked up the crossbow, and threw it into the shrubbery before giving the Brigadier an unchristian kick in the head before crossing to the inconsolable Joe, who was standing in the middle of the path over the dead body of his beloved dog with the still-smoking blunderbuss lying at his feet.

"I fired too late to stop that bastard shooting my poor old Rex." He sobbed with tears running freely down his cheeks.

Bill turned to Anne and helped her to her feet, but not before reaching down to retrieve the yawara stick from where it lay beside the still-screaming Ophelia.

"Let's return to the vicarage; Ron and Mary may require our assistance.

Joe, if you could assist Anne, I will carry Rex." Bill told the still-grieving Joe as he stooped to pick up the unfortunate dog.

"What about them?" Asked Anne, indicating the bleeding Brigadier and wailing Ophelia.

"They can stay here and suffer for all I care," Bill replied in what some people may consider morally wrong for a vicar, but he was past caring by this time and calling Duchess and Archie from amongst the trees where they had been hiding since the shot from the blunderbuss.

As they left the two suffering killers, Anne had the presence of mind to pick up Joe's blunderbuss in passing.

"How come you came to our rescue when you did?" Bill asked Joe as they hurried back in the direction of the village.

"Rex and I were out in the yard when you passed, and then his tail stopped wagging, and he began growling.

When I looked up, I saw the Brigadier and that bitch of a wife of his following you and carrying that crossbow.

After my bang on the head, I began trusting Rex's instincts more, and when he growled at the Beauchamps, I knew that all was not well, so I went into the house for the blunderbuss and followed, arriving in time to hear them admitting to you how they committed those three murders.

Do you think it was Ophelia who attacked me that day in the shed?"

Almost certainly, because she felt that you had belittled the Brigadier the other day at the Manor by not removing the gypsies from your field, and if Rex hadn't attacked her when he did, you wouldn't have been here now and come to that, neither would we."

CHAPTER 18

The Aftermath
Saturday evening

Approaching the vicarage, they saw Inspector Doyle's black Rover parked at the gate, and they were unsure whether that was a good or a bad omen.

From the corner of his eye, Bill saw Anne drop the blunderbuss into the thick foliage of the privet hedge where it would be away from prying eyes.

Entering the porch of the vicarage, Bill laid the unfortunate Rex on top of the leather-topped box seat.

A smiling Ron met them as they made their way to the kitchen. "Typical; you two pop out for an hour, and all hell breaks loose here." Then he saw Joe's tear-streaked cheeks and Anne covered in dust and limping before rushing forward to take her arm and steered her towards the kitchen, where he sat her beside Mary.

Joe and Bill followed Ron to find Inspector Doyle, PC Gregory and a bloody-faced Hopkins standing by the sink whilst Mary was seated at the table nursing a glass of whisky.

"You all right?" Bill said to his sister, placing a reassuring hand on her shoulder.

She gave a feeble smile and a thumbs-up before taking another sip of her whisky.

Turning to Ron, Bill indicated Hopkins and said, "Did you do that?"

He smiled and nodded towards Mary and said, "Nope, she did the honours."

Turning to Hopkins, Bill said, "A girl beat you up. What will Ophelia say to that?"

"The bitch broke my dose." He mumbled through the blood before PC Gregory elbowed him in the stomach and told him to watch his language.

"What happened?" Bill asked Ron.

"Not long after you and Anne had left, there was a knock at the door, and Mary went to answer it whilst I stayed in the kitchen with the ledger.

I heard their voices in the hallway, and then Mary came in with Hopkins holding a gun to her head. I got to my feet, and as he turned the gun towards me, Mary snapped her head back, breaking his nose, followed by stamping upon his foot and planting an elbow in his gut, causing him to double over, during which I grabbed his wrist, twisted it and relieved him of his gun."

Bill turned to his sister and said, "Well done, little sister. Your old training may have saved your lives because the Brigadier informed us not twenty minutes ago that he had ordered Hopkins to kill Ron and yourself before stealing the ledger."

Even the Inspector appeared shocked by his

statement and said, "Why would he tell you this?"

"Because the Brigadier and his wife said they were going to kill Doctor Clements and me and leave our burnt bodies in the ashes of the Manor.

Thanks to Mr Ross and his dog Rex, whose timely intervention saved us from the Brigadier and Ophelia, we escaped. Alas, Rex was unfortunately killed in our rescue by the Brigadier."

"What is in the ledger that Brigadier Beauchamp did not want you to reveal?" Asked the Inspector.

"We don't know yet as we have not got around to decoding its contents, but I think it may have something to do with his past, and this afternoon, if they had known we had just discovered Micky's photographs hidden in an old hollow oak tree in the woods, I think they would have killed us on the spot.

I left them on the hall table on my way in; I will get them for you."

As Bill left the room, Anne gave him a questioning look, to which he shook his head slightly in reply.

Once in the hall and out of sight, he removed the envelope from his waistband and sifted through the photos and negatives before removing all those referring to the young girl whose family had paid money to Micky before leaving the village. Bill gathered and buried them in the hall table drawer under some letters before replacing the remainder in the envelope.

Returning to the kitchen, he handed the envelope to the Inspector and regained his seat at the table next to Anne.

The first photograph the Inspector took out of the envelope was of Ophelia and Hopkins, and his eyebrows shot up.

Looking over the Inspector's shoulder, Ron let out a "Bloody Nora" and glanced at Hopkins, who, realising what was in the picture, surprisingly blushed.

The Inspector hurriedly placed the photograph back in the envelope before tucking it into his jacket pocket.

"Gregory, take him to the police house and lock him up. Tell PC Day to watch him, and we will collect you on our way to the woods, " The Inspector ordered.

"Mr Clements and the vicar will accompany me to the woods, and Mr Ross, I would like you to stay here with the ladies.

As they left the vicarage, Bill took the time to cover the remains of poor old Rex with a jacket and say a short prayer over him.

"I thought the church didn't believe animals had souls?" Asked the Inspector as they left.

"I don't know if animals have souls, but I think that if heaven is such a wonderful place as we believe it to be, it must have the animals that have given us so much love,"

After a brief stop at the police house to collect PC Gregory, they made their way to the woods, where Bill led them to the spot on the path where he had left the Brigadier and Ophelia to find Django Lee standing in the clearing.

"Hello, Mr Lee." Said the Inspector, "What are you doing here?"

"We heard the woman screaming from our camp, and I came across in time to see the Brigadier and his wife leaving; they both looked in a bad way, with him covered in blood and her trying to hold him up.

I went to help, and all I got was what I assumed to be abuse, but as she was talking in what I thought to be German, I couldn't understand, so I kept my distance."

Bill retrieved the crossbow from where it was still lying in the bushes where he had thrown it, and in the dust were what looked like numerous droplets of blood.

The trail of blood led from the woods before disappearing in the long grass of the hay field.

"Where now?" Enquired Ron.

Bill turned to the Inspector, who looked about and said, "I think from what Mr Lee said, they will be making their way back to the Manor hoping for a clean getaway, so I suggest we start there." So, without hesitation, they returned to the Rover and set off back through the village and toward the Manor.

Halfway along the tree-lined driveway to the Manor, the police car met a man and woman waving their arms for them to stop.

"That's Amos Tennent and Mrs Moore, "said Ron, "they work at the Manor."

The Inspector brought the Rover to a halt alongside the waving couple and wound down his window.

Before the Inspector could say a word, Mrs Moore said. "Vicar, what on earth is happening? The poor Brigadier is covered in blood and told us to leave the house."

"Yes, and the Mrs is babbling away in German. I learnt a bit of the language in the First War, and what she said wasn't very polite, I can tell you," butted in Amos.

"Mrs Moore and Mr Tennent go home and don't return to the Manor." Said Bill. "Until the police tell you it is safe."

"Who are they?" asked the Inspector as they left the bemused couple looking nervously over their shoulders.

"They are the cook and gamekeeper," said Ron, "And I reckon they were lucky to get out of the Manor alive."

Reaching the Manor, they found Ophelia cradling the second crossbow before the wide-open door leading into the study.

"Spread out," said the Inspector in hushed tones as he calmly stepped over the threshold and said to Ophelia, "Lady Beauchamp, please lower the crossbow as I wish to ask you a few questions relating to the deaths of Micky Jordan, Kathy Jordan and Sergeant Humphrey Wilson."

Ophelia showed no change in her blank facial expression as she levelled the crossbow at the

Inspector and said in a dull monotone, "Leave my house now, or I will kill you." Entering the hallway, Bill moved to the Inspector's left while Ron and PC Gregory spread out to his right.

Ophelia's crossbow wavered from side to side as they edged forward.

Over Ophelia's shoulder, Bill could see the Brigadier slumped in his desk chair, holding what looked like a Luger pistol in a blood-soaked right hand, watching the unfolding events in the Manor. Even more sickening was their three dogs lying on the study floor in front of the desk in pools of blood with their throats cut.

Bill, remembering Ophelias' aversion to loud noises, pretended to stumble and stepped to his left before the crossbow could point in his direction and kicked out at the suit of armour, which in turn toppled onto the brass dinner gong, creating a cacophony, causing Ophelia, to drop the crossbow which upon striking the floor fired the bolt into the door frame between Bill and the Inspector.

As Ophelia, for the second time that day, lay on the floor writhing and screaming in pain from her hyperacusis, they started to move forward to overpower the Brigadier.

But somehow, the Brigadier found the strength to stagger to his feet and stumble from his study whilst keeping Bill and the others at bay with his pistol.

He knelt beside his wailing wife and, still keeping

the others at a safe distance, stroked her hair and said, "Mein liebes Mädchen," pointed the gun at her temple and pulled the trigger.

With the explosion of the shot, everyone became rooted to the spot. As the Brigadier started to turn the gun upon himself, Ron reacted first by diving forward and knocking the pistol from the Brigadier's grasp before wrestling him to the floor. He cried in anguish, "Nein, nein, let me die." The Inspector and PC Gregory pinned him to the floor before restraining him with handcuffs and dragging the struggling, broken figure towards the Rover; with his blood-soaked shirt and dishevelled hair, it was hard to imagine this sobbing man as the same sophisticated, smartly dressed Brigadier they had come to know, but why was he speaking German?

"Reverend," said the Inspector, "If it is all right with you, I would like to take him back to the vicarage so that Doctor Clements can dress his wounds."

"By all means, Inspector, Mr Clements and I will remain here with the body until you can send someone to take over."

CHAPTER 19

Discoveries
Late Saturday

After the Inspector and PC Gregory had departed with the bleeding Brigadier in the Rover, Ron and Bill covered the dogs and Ophelia's remains with blankets from the Brigadier's study and then decided to look around the Manor while waiting for the police to return.

Bill started by going up the stairs, and the first door he opened was to a bathroom. He smiled as he thought of Kathy Jordan's prefab with its coal in the bath and imagined Ophelia letting there be a dirty mark on her bath, let alone filling it with coal.

He continued his search of the upstairs, but there was nothing out of the ordinary, just bedrooms and another bathroom, which he thought would be handy in the vicarage as he and Mary were constantly squabbling over him, leaving the toilet seat up.

Making his way back down the stairs to the hallway, he went through a side door to the library and found himself in a games room with a full-size snooker table.

He was getting ready to set up the balls for a game while they waited when Ron shouted, "Bill, you have to come and see this."

Bill went across the hall to the Brigadier's study, where there was no sign of Ron; he called out Ron's name only to see a door suddenly open in the bookcase, and Ron appeared, saying,

"You have to come and look at this."

Going through the hidden door, Bill found himself in a small room about twelve feet across, but its decor was the fantastic thing about the room.

Hanging on one wall was a large red, black and white flag with a swastika in the centre. On a desk in front of the flag was a collection of black and white photographs along with two SS daggers, one of which must have been the one he had seen on the Brigadier's desk the day he had visited. Looking back into the study, he saw he was correct; the dagger was no longer in sight.

On either side of the flag stood two manakins dressed in black SS uniforms, one male and one female.

The holster of the male uniform was open and empty, explaining where the Brigadier had acquired his Luger.

Upon another wall was a portrait of Adolf Hitler surrounded by even more photographs, some of which were in colour.

Turning to Ron, he said, "What have we come across here, some sort of sick game playing?"

"I think it's worse than that." Said Ron, "Look closely at some of the colour photographs beside Hitler's portrait."

Looking closer at the colour photographs, he asked Ron, "What am I looking for?"

"Look to see whom Hitler is shaking hands with."

Looking closer, Bill almost fainted with shock. "Oh my God, it's the Brigadier and Ophelia wearing SS uniforms; that explains how come the Brigadier spoke German, but how can this be? How did they get from being SS officers to a local land owner here in Kent?"

As they looked at the other photographs, they were again in two, standing and smiling at the camera outside the gates   of what appeared to be two concentration camps with their retched inmates peering through the wire.

Taking one of the photos, Bill slipped it into his pocket to show the others when they returned to the vicarage.

The photos were nothing compared to what he found in the second desk drawers he opened.

The first thing he spied was Micky's camera lying on top of some documents written in German, which neither of them could read, but at the bottom of the pile were two identity cards with the names Hector and Ophelia Beauchamp, which were printed in English this time.

One described Hector Beauchamp as sixty-five years old, five feet nine inches tall, fifteen stone in weight, of stocky build with brown hair and green eyes.

The second identity card described Ophelia Beauchamp as fifty-nine years old, five feet ten inches tall, eight stone three pounds weight, of slim build with blonde hair and blue eyes.

The photographs on the two cards showed a round-faced man with a receding hairline and an attractive woman with long blonde hair.

Taking a closer look at the pictures of the two unknown people, Ron said, "If the people in the photographs are the real Brigadier and Ophelia, I don't rate their chances of still being alive after they ran into this murderous pair, and I think this would be best left to the authorities as we are getting well out of our depth with."

Replacing the identity cards and papers into the drawer, they made their way through to the library, where they made themselves comfortable in a pair of well-stuffed armchairs to await the police and, seeing as the Brigadier was in no condition to object, made inroads into a rather fine bottle of his malt whisky that Ron had discovered on the drinks trolley.

As they sat swopping war stories and the level on the whisky bottle went down, Ron suddenly said, "Do you ever have nightmares about some of the things you saw during the war?"

"How could we not after some of the things we have seen? If I can get through a week without waking up at least one night in a clammy sweat. And you?"

"I'm the same; some of the sights on that beach of men and parts of men laying in the sand, and all you could do is ignore the screams for help and keep moving forward. I asked Bert the same question one evening in the pub, and he said that he had one recurring nightmare. His squad had been put ashore on a small island off the French coast with instructions to destroy a German E-boat flotilla that had been reported as causing a lot of trouble in the channel, attacking fishing boats on the South coast.

All had gone well; they had disposed of the sentries and planted their timed charges on the boats when Bert heard the new Lieutenant cry out in pain. He had seemingly slipped from the boat deck where he was placing his explosive charge and fell to the dock.

And that was where Bert discovered the poor bugger impaled on an upright rusty piece of angle iron.

The young officer was not dead but, though in severe pain, had managed to tell Bert and the others to leave because he knew when the charges exploded, his distress would end.

Bert had told me that he would never forget the courage of that young officer who hadn't made a sound throughout his agony and given away their position.

Like you and me, he still awoke during the night, remembering that young man's courage.

I maybe shouldn't be telling you this, but Anne

also has her nightmares; it was during the blitz that she and the other student doctors were being called upon to assist with the casualties.

Anne had gone out in one of the ambulances to some tenements in the East End that had suffered severe bomb damage.

When she arrived, the rescuers had recently finished digging into the rubble to reach the tenement residents who had taken shelter in the cellar.

Getting from the ambulance, she approached the warden in charge of the rescue, who shook his head and informed her that she could do nothing. She said there must be someone alive, although injured. He told her that the bomb that had blocked the exit from the cellar also caused a water pipe to fracture, flooding the basement and drowning all the occupants who had been unable to make their escape.

She says to this day, she still can't enter confined spaces as she imagines the panic and fear of those poor people as the water slowly rose."

"We sometimes forgot while we were away that the people at home suffered the same as us, sometimes worse as they had no way to fight back." Said Bill, taking another drink.

CHAPTER 20
The Message From the Blotter
Later Saturday

It was an hour before anyone arrived, and it was in the form of Sergeant Cornwell, accompanied by four constables, a photographer and a civilian police surgeon, as it was a legal requirement that the doctor confirm Ophelia was dead.

It didn't matter that half her face was missing; the law is the law.

Before leaving the Manor, they took Sergeant Cornwell through to the hidden room and no sooner had he seen the contents than he was on the radio in the police car to inform Inspector Doyle of their discovery.

Leaving the police to get on with their investigations, they returned to the vicarage to discover that the last two members of the Dog Walkers Society had arrived and were all sitting around the table in the kitchen.

Mary and Anne met them at the door with hugs and kisses and asked why we had been so long.

They explained about the police and the doctor taking their time and pulling the Brigadier's bottle of malt from his pocket; Ron said, "Where do you keep the glasses?"

Mary answered scornfully, "Ron Clements, that is stealing. You should be ashamed of yourself, and you will find them in the corner cupboard beside the sink."

"That isn't all we removed," Bill said, took a photograph from his pocket, and laid it on the kitchen table.

The intake of breath was so great that he was surprised there was air left in the kitchen when they saw the picture of the Brigadier with Hitler.

When they thought they couldn't be more surprised, Ron told them about the two identity cards and the two people in the photographs.

The ringing telephone broke the stunned silence. Bill went to the study to answer it and discovered it to be Sam Peters, the Reverend Peters's nephew, calling to inform him that his uncle was awake and would like to see him the next day at Dartford Hospital.

Bill said that he would be there after the morning service, and he was to tell his uncle that the West Kent Dog Wakers Society had made a few discoveries of their own.

Returning to the kitchen, he gave the others the good news and said he would like to decode some of the pages in the ledger before leaving for Dartford tomorrow.

"Ah, we are way ahead of you there. While you and my brother were sitting in comfort swigging the

Brigadier's best malt, Mary and I started decoding the sheet you discovered in the blotter, which is fascinating, too." Said Anne.

"Come on, spit it out; what did you discover?" Said Ron to his smiling sibling.

"Well, that sheet was dated Sunday, before his attack, and we think that he was typing it when his attacker, i.e. Ophelia, arrived at his house and, not having time to store it in the ledger, hid it in his blotter."

"What had he written before he was interrupted?" Bill asked, and Anne laid out the decoded sheet on the kitchen table to see.

Sunday 7th June 1953

I am leaving this message in the blotter rather than the ledger in case something should happen to me.

The day before I moved to Eynsford, I received a letter from my good friend Rabbi Silverstein, whom I'd had the pleasure of meeting last year at a dinner party we had both attended in London.

During the conversations of the evening, I had mentioned to him that I lived in the village of Lower Dipping in Kent. He said that was a coincidence as he had an old friend from South Africa who had purchased the Manor House in Lower Dipping sight unseen. He planned to move there upon his retirement after the war, and maybe I had heard of him; his name is Hector Beauchamp.

I said, amazingly, I did as I was the vicar of the village where he lived, and the Brigadier was one of the leading lights in the community.

As the evening progressed, Silverstein told me about his life in South Africa and one story, in particular; there had been a spate of burglaries in his town, so he had purchased a Rhodesian Ridgeback guard dog to protect his property and, to his surprise, from that day onwards, Hector never revisited his house.

When Silverstein had asked his friend why he no longer called, Beauchamp told him that as a child, he had been bitten by his aunt's corgi and, from that day to this, had been terrified of dogs.

I thought it strange about the dogs, as the Brigadier I knew had two labradors, but it could have been that he was afraid of Rhodesian Ridgebacks and didn't want to offend his friend.

I heard no more from Silverstein after that night until I received the letter I mentioned earlier that said he was arriving in Eynsford for a visit on Saturday, 30th May and thought he would stop off on the way at the Manor to see the Beauchamps for himself, but that was the last I heard from him as he never arrived.

Picking up the sheet of paper, Anne said, "That was where it stopped, and we surmised that it was at this point Ophelia arrived, struck the reverend with her Yawara stick and left him for dead at the foot of his stairs to make it look like an accident."

"Did you get a chance to decipher more of the

ledger?" Bill asked, taking another sip of his malt whisky.

"Not much," said Mary, "we thought we would start at the end and work backwards, but the only bit of interest that we found was where the reverend had asked something called The Box to look into the background of the Brigadier and Ophelia, but as we don't know what The Box is, it's not much help."

Gathering the sheets of paper and photographs, Bill took them to the study and locked them in the ancient grey safe alongside the parish records.

Returning to the kitchen, the remaining West Kent Dog Walkers Society members sat around the table or leaned against the wall, holding their topped-up glasses.

"Glad to see you've all got more drinks while I was gone," Bill said, spying the Brigadier's empty bottle of malt on the draining board.

Seeing his crestfallen expression, they all laughed, and Ron reached behind the teapot to produce Bill's newly filled glass.

Taking the glass, Bill raised it and said, "I think we should all drink to the hero of the day. Rex."

Everyone raised their glasses and chorused, "Rex." Draining their glasses.

Bill drained his glass and said. "Now we know what caused the start of the murders; it was Rabbi Silverstein arriving at the Manor. I think that he must have given himself away at some point, and they killed him, and I'm certain the police will locate his body hidden somewhere on the grounds of the Manor."

The gathering of members went on for another two hours before breaking up, and everyone went to their respective homes except for Joe, who was taken back to the Mucky Duck by Bert for a few more drinks and to help him get over the death of his dog.

***

It was six in the morning when Mary and Bill, awakened by a frantic banging on the vicarage door, had set the dogs to barking.

Putting on his dressing gown, he descended the stairs and opened the door to discover a white-faced PC Gregory.

"Thank God you are both safe," he said as he spied Mary behind the vicar standing on the stairs.

"What on earth has happened?" Bill asked.

"Hopkins has escaped."

"The inspector won't like that," Bill replied, "he will have Constable Day's guts for garters."

"He will have a job because Hopkins killed him in the escape; when I came on duty just now, I found Jack Days' body in Hopkins's cell with his head caved in and his bloody truncheon laying beside the body."

It was Bill's turn to turn white, and he said. "Did you phone the inspector?"

"Yes, luckily, he was still at Maidstone HQ after spending the night interviewing the Brigadier; he said he would bring help as quickly as possible, and

I was to check that you and your sister were okay, and then I was to check on Doctor Clements and her brother."

Bill told Mary what had happened and that she was to stay in the house with the doors locked while he and Dave Gregory went to check on Anne and Ron. "Not on your life. Am I staying here on my own? You're forgetting who gave him a broken nose. Just give me a minute to throw on some clothes."

By the time Dave Gregory had left Lower Dipping House, two police vans full of officers and Inspector Doyles Rover had arrived in the village and had begun their search for Hopkins.

CHAPTER 21

Reverend Peters Tells His Story
Sunday 14th

After morning service, Ron, Mary, Anne and Bill piled again into Anne's Hillman and set off to Dartford to meet with the Reverend Peters.

"Do you think the Reverend Peters will be able to tell us much about the background of the Brigadier and Ophelia?" Said Anne from beside Bill at the wheel.

"I don't know," Bill replied, "Everything we have discovered so far has been by sheer luck. Not any great deductive reasoning."

"That's not true." Said, Ron,

"Who saw no mud on the stairs in the vicarage the night of Micky's death? It was you.

Who was it discovered the charred remains of the picture in the grate and the image of the oak tree on the wall of the prefab? It was you, and you discovered just a few things in the hunt for Micky's killer.

Indeed, you weren't alone, and other people helped, but the information was gathered from you, acting as the nucleus.

Now stop being so modest and decide where you will buy us lunch on returning home."

"Where on earth did you learn to use the word nucleus in its correct context?" Asked his sister.

"If you must know, Dan Dare used it in last week's Eagle comic," Ron smiled. "Now concentrate on your driving."

Upon their arrival at the hospital, after an enjoyable drive through the sunny Kent countryside, they made their way up the stairs to the men's ward, they were confronted at the door by a formidable ward sister who told them they couldn't visit the Reverend Peters at this time as it was outside visiting hours and he already had two visitors. Although he was in a private room, four more were likely to cause him far too much distress.

Stepping forward, Anne took the lead and assured the sister in her most charming manner that the reverend had requested their visit and as she was a doctor and as he already had two visitors, four more were unlikely to cause him any distress. If she noticed that the reverend was tiring or getting distressed for any reason during the visit, she would end the stay immediately and call for the sister at once.

Mary, Ron and Bill looked on in stunned amazement at seeing Anne in this full doctor mode, having never seen it before.

The ward sister looked them over with steely eyes, took a deep breath, gave them another long look without saying a word, sniffed loudly and disappeared into her office.

They located and entered the reverend's room to find him sitting in bed, looking like an Indian Raja with a bandage wrapped around his head like a turban and white hair poking through the crown, similar to a feathered plume.

As they entered, the reverend gave a welcoming smile, and the two men seated on either side of the bed started to get to their feet, reaching inside their jackets until they saw they were no threat.

Bill recognised the younger of the two as Sam Peters and assumed the older man to be his father due to his familiar appearance to the reverend.

"Afternoon, David; glad you are looking more like your old self," Bill said, stepping to one side of the door to let the others enter.

"Good to see you as well, Bill; I'm sorry to have caused you so much trouble, especially with Sergeant Wilson. I had no idea he was related to Micky or so pally with the Brigadier until it was too late, and I had sent you those letters, or I would have warned you."

The girls took the two remaining chairs whilst Ron and Bill leaned against the wall on either side of the door.

"It's not your fault that the Brigadier and Ophelia are a pair of psychopaths," Bill said.

"I should never have sent you those warning letters, for as soon as you showed them to the Brigadier, he decided upon your removal as he was unsure of how much you knew,

But before I carry on with my tale, I had better introduce my brother Frank and his son Sam, who I believe Bill is the only one to have met. They have kindly come to sit with me until the police find that man Hopkins."

"That will explain the conspicuous bulges spoiling the cut of their jackets." Said Ron seriously.

"Well spotted, Mr Clements," said Sam, "and when you get home, you will find some more men at your homes similarly attired."

"Who are you people exactly?" Asked Anne. "Other than the reverend's relatives."

Looking at his father, Sam received a nod of consent.

Turning to Anne, Sam smiled and said, "We jokingly call it the family firm as Uncle David sometimes helps out and Dad and I are full-time members, though I am still a junior member of Box 500 or MI5 as it is properly known."

"Why Box 500?" Asked Anne.

"Because in its early days, it was so secret that was its only postal address." Said a smiling Sam.

At that moment, the Reverend Peters said, "Right, anyway, I had better get on before that terrifying ward sister returns. It all began after the party in London. I understand you all know about it as you discovered the paper I hid in the blotter, and you deciphered its contents, which was very clever of you all.

Sorry, I'm going off track, and after my

conversation with Rabbi Silverstein in London, I asked Frank to dig into the backgrounds of the Brigadier and Ophelia. Tell them what you found, Frank."

Frank Peters turned to face us, settled in his chair, and began his tale.

"Hector and Ophelia Beauchamp had a comfortable life in India between the two wars. Hector was not a fighting soldier but an organiser and a very efficient one.

If the movement of essential war supplies back to the UK was required, Hector was the man to get it done, and it was this that had him transferred from India to South Africa to organise the movement of essential war supplies back to the United Kingdom.

At the war's end, Hector decided it was time for him to retire and return home to England aboard the SS Durban Star.

It was during the journey from Cape Town to the United Kingdom that the Durban Star had a stopover in Lisbon, and this is where we think your Brigadier and Ophelia murdered the real Beauchamps and stole their identities before continuing to the UK aboard another ship with their new names.

Whilst we suspected that Hector and Ophelia weren't who they said they were and that they murdered Rabbi Silverstein, we had no proof until yesterday when you discovered the secret room with their true identities."

"Who are they?" Asked Mary.

"They are Heinrich and Greta Klein and two of the most truly evil people you will come across and high on the list of wanted war criminals." Answered Frank, his face showing the disgust he felt at even having to mention their names.

"They are not a married couple as they pretended to be to you but a brother and sister who were part of Hitler's elite that ran slave labour camps in Poland for their Fuhrer during the war.

Heinrich and Greta were renowned for their cruelty and depravities towards the inmates, the details of which I shall not go into.

Now that we have Heinrich in custody and before transporting him back to Germany, we will persuade him to tell us what happened to the genuine Hector and Ophelia and what they did to Rabbi Silverstein, whose remains we eventually found in an old disused well on the grounds of the Manor. The poor man had not died well, as he had undergone very severe torture, the details of which I do not want to go into."

"Surely he can be prosecuted for his crimes in this country?" Bill asked.

"In this country, we have no proof that he killed anyone; all he has to say is that it was his sister who committed the murders, but in Germany, he will be tried for his war crimes."

"What about Hopkins, and how does he fit into the scenario?" Asked Mary.

"From what we can find out about George Edward

Hopkins, he is no more than hired muscle. He was born at the end of the First World War in London's East End, where, in the Thirties, he joined The British Union of Fascists as one of the Blackshirts led by Oswald Mosley.

He only came to our attention after being arrested during the battle of Cable Street in nineteen thirty-six when Mosley tried to march through the Jewish quarter of the East End. The Kleins must have had some Fascist contacts here in Britain who put them in touch with Hopkins, who they used to do any dirty work."

As Frank was coming to the end of his tale, the door slammed into the wall beside Bill, and there, framed in the doorway, stood Hopkins, pointing a pistol at arm's length directly at David Peters as he lay in his bed.

"You interfering, old bastard." He roared, and as he started to squeeze the trigger, Ron kicked the underside of his arm, causing the gun to fire into the ceiling.

Bill dived across the room to protect Anne and knocked her from her chair out of the line of fire as the room shook from the double explosions of the MI5 agents' guns.

The ward sister, having just left her office, gave a startled squeak as Hopkins was thrown into the corridor to land at her feet, pumping blood from the two bullet wounds in his chest; the two MI5 agents followed, still holding their smoking revolvers.

As Bill lay shielding Anne with his body, he felt pain shoot up his leg and realised that he had injured his ankle in his dive to protect her.

That's typical; he thought to have jumped out of umpteen aeroplanes during the war without so much as a minor sprain, and now he had injured his ankle diving across a room.

As Anne recovered from her shock, she pushed Bill, who was still covering her body with his own roughly, to one side only to realise all was not well as he groaned.

Turning to face him, she told him to lay still as she ripped open his shirt in her search for bullet holes, and it wasn't until he managed to tell her that it was only a sprained ankle that she slapped him and said, "You stupid bastard I thought he had shot you," and then kissed him.

When she had eventually removed her lips from his, a smiling Ron helped Bill to his feet and sat him in the chair alongside the reverend's bed.

"Joe's right, Bill; for a vicar, you don't half swear a lot, and now you have got my sister swearing as well."

Turning to the Reverend Peters, he said. "Reverend, I must apologise for the improper language you have just heard."

"That's all right, my son. I learnt much bad language during the First World War and learned it can be a right bastard of a shock when the bullets start flying." The elderly smiling vicar replied.

The door opened, and the two MI5 men returned to

the room. "Are you all okay?"

"At last," said Mary, glowering at Ron and her brother whilst crawling from under the bed where she had dived when the bullets had begun to fly. "Someone is asking how I am."

After the two MI5 men had gone to arrange with the police the removal of Hopkin's body down to the mortuary, Ron said to his sister, "How is our wounded soldier?"

"He has a severely sprained ankle, and don't you be bad to him. He was fearless in trying to protect me."

"Has he hurt his arm?"

"No, why?"

"I just wanted to make sure he can still reach for his wallet to buy our lunch on the way home." Said Ron, ducking a wild swipe from his sister.

After strapping Bill's sprained ankle and saying farewells to the Reverend Peters and his family, they promised to exchange stories when he got home to Eynsford; they returned to the car with Bill leaning on a crutch that Ron said he had found lying around in the corridor.

EPILOGUE

It had been two weeks since the shooting at the hospital, and the West Kent Dog Walkers were meeting in the Lounge Bar of the Mucky Duck with a couple of Honorary guests.

The group agreed that Ron should take the chair for the first meeting and that the chair would then rotate with a new chairperson at each session.

Ron rapped on the table and said. "Ladies and gentlemen, welcome to the new West Kent Dog Walkers Society, and I would like to welcome our two honoured guests, The Reverend David Peters from Eynsford, who was kindly brought over to Lower Dipping by Tractor Tom, who, besides owning a tractor is also Eynsford's only Taxi service and secondly our very own Constable Dave Gregory who has assured us that for the next meeting, he will borrow his land ladies dog until he can acquire one of his own."

There was another rap on the table, and Miss Harlan stood up and said, "Point of order, Mister Chairman, as Mr Joe Ross no longer has a dog after the brave demise of his Rex, how can he remain a member of the Dog Walkers Society?"

"That is an excellent point, Miss Harlan, and what does Mr Ross have to say on the subject?"

Joe looked shocked and said. "Mr Chairman, it is not something to which I have given any thought, but as it is The Dog Walkers Society and I have no dog, then I must leave," and he started to get to his feet.

"One moment, please, Mr Ross." Said Ron and nodded to Elsie, who went through to the Public Bar and, as she came back, gave Ron a nod in return as the door opened.

Tractor Tom came into the room carrying a cardboard box, which he handed to Ron, who in turn passed it to Joe and said, "As a sign of appreciation from us all for all your assistance at the coronation party in acquiring the marquees and in recognition of Rex's bravery, we would like to introduce you to Queenie. Whereas before you had a king, you can now have a queen."

Joe opened the box and gave a broad smile as he lifted out a small wriggling black and tan Jack Russell puppy who immediately licked the end of his nose.

Wiping away a tear, he said, "Thank you all so much; I don't know what to say."

A chorus of voices declared, "I'll buy the drinks!" in response to his question.

Before Elsie could pour the drinks, the door swung open, Inspector Doyle entered the room, and silence fell. Dave Gregory leapt to his feet before being waved back down again by the Inspector, who said, "Sorry to interrupt your meeting, but I have just received a message from Maidstone prison that Heinrich Klein was found dead in his cell this evening. It appears he had taken poison, though it is unknown how it found its way into his possession."

The room sat stunned until Joe got to his feet and called across to the bar, "Elsie, make those drinks doubles and one for the Inspector."

ABOUT THE AUTHOR

Bob Charles

I was born in Kent in 1950 and vaguely recalled being lifted over the garden fence by my Father to watch the Coronation on a neighbour's television with its nine-inch screen.

Lower Dipping is an imaginary village, but Eynsford, complete with, ford is genuine.

Eynsford may have had a Tractor Tom in 1953, but if not, it should have had.

BC

Printed in Great Britain
by Amazon